SHADOWS OF MY ENEMY
THE SAMUEL CLAYTON FILES

By Scott Danville

This book is based on real events.

DANVILLE
HOUSE
BOOKS
Words That Matter

Published by Danville House Books,
an imprint of Danville House Publishing

ISBN: 979-8-9986320-0-6

Printed in the United States of America

First Edition

Dedication

To the woman I love, Diana Danville.

For your unwavering support, belief in me, and the love that transcends all shadows. You are my light.

Table of Contents

Prologue
Moscow, 1993

A bitter wind cut across Red Square as Richard Kessler adjusted his overcoat, the fur collar offering little protection against the Russian winter. Two years after the Soviet collapse, Moscow remained a city of shadows and whispers, where former KGB officers reinvented themselves as businessmen overnight and state secrets transformed into private commodities.

"The files are complete?" Kessler asked, his breath forming clouds in the frozen air.

Dmitri Volkov nodded once, his expression unreadable behind tinted glasses. "Everything from the climate monitoring stations across Siberia, just as you requested. Thirty years of data the West never saw."

What Volkov didn't mention was that the records had been systematically altered before reaching Kessler's hands – temperature readings subtly modified, precipitation patterns adjusted, ice measurements recalibrated. Small changes, scientifically plausible, but creating a pattern that served specific interests when incorporated into global climate models.

"The Americans suspect nothing?" Volkov asked.

"They're still celebrating winning the Cold War," Kessler replied, his tone dismissive. "They see what they expect to see."

Not all Americans, of course. Even then, Kessler knew about the small network of analysts who had detected anomalies in Soviet climate data during the 1980s. Individuals with particular cognitive frameworks that allowed them to recognize manipulated patterns. People like Samuel Clayton, whose father's CIA connections had placed him on monitoring lists since his first remarkable science project on Arctic temperature variations.

"And our mutual associates?" Volkov pressed.

Kessler's expression hardened. "They understand the long-term value of controlling environmental data. Resource allocation, market advantages, policy leverage – all flow from who controls the baseline measurements."

What began that day would evolve over decades into what intelligence agencies would later call the Consortium – not an organization exactly, but a network of influential individuals using climate science as a mechanism for unprecedented market manipulation.

Neither man noticed the slender figure on the opposite side of the square, camera disguised as a tourist's souvenir. Phoebe MacReynolds had been tracking Kessler's movements since his suspicious resignation from government service. The photographs she took that day would eventually reach her son, by then a young teacher with no knowledge of his family's intelligence connections.

The true implications would take years to fully emerge – a shadow war fought with data instead of weapons, where the ability to recognize manipulated patterns determined who controlled the future of global resources.

And in the center of it all, unknowingly: a young family in Plattsburgh, where an earth science teacher named Sam Clayton was about to discover that the line between teacher and operative, husband and agent, father and target, was far thinner than he ever imagined.

Chapter 1
A Ghost in Copenhagen
October 2009

Steam rose from the cobblestones as Sam Clayton crossed Kongens Nytorv Square, his breath visible in the October chill. Copenhagen embraced autumn differently than upstate New York—the darkness descended earlier, the air carried hints of the Baltic, and something else hung in the atmosphere tonight. Something wrong.

Sam checked his watch—11:42 PM—as he navigated around a cluster of bicycles. The International Secondary Education Teachers' Conference had wrapped its second day, his presentation on climate data collection methodologies receiving unexpected attention from several attendees who asked questions far too precise for typical educators.

Behind him, Tivoli Gardens had closed hours ago, its fairytale turrets now just silhouettes against the night sky. His mother's words from this morning echoed in his mind: "The patterns are shifting, Samuel." Phoebe MacReynolds never wasted words, especially during operations. At sixty-seven, she maintained the precise diction of her academic cover, even when delivering warnings.

Inside his jacket pocket, a flash drive contained data anomalies that shouldn't exist—variations in weather buoy readings across three continents that followed no natural pattern. The discovery had been accidental, a careless mistake by someone manipulating the baseline measurements. Someone controlling the narrative around changing sea temperatures.

Sam paused at the street corner, ostensibly checking his conference schedule. In reality, he scanned reflections in shop windows, counting the figures that had maintained consistent distance since he left the Admiral Hotel. Three operatives, moving with too much purpose for random tourists. One positioned at his ten o'clock, another across the square, the third trailing behind. Professional surveillance.

While dozens of teachers from around the world discussed classroom strategies, something darker unfolded beneath Copenhagen's charming exterior.

"You must try the jazz club tonight, Professor Clayton," Dr. Anders Magnussen had urged over lunch. The Norwegian climatologist's enthusiasm seemed genuine, his shock of white hair bouncing as he handed Sam a business card for The Standard. "Copenhagen after dark—it speaks to the soul differently."

The Europeans' tendency to address secondary educators as 'Professor' had always served Sam's cover well, lending his teacher identity just enough academic weight to access research circles without scrutiny.

Anders had shared concerning findings about anomalies in North Sea temperature readings— patterns that echoed what Sam had detected in his own research. Too consistent to be natural, too widespread to be equipment malfunction.

"Data doesn't lie," Anders had said, his voice dropping. "But people manipulating data—they have agendas."

Now, seven hours later, Sam pushed through the heavy oak door of The Standard, jazz spilling onto the street. The club occupied the ground floor of a 1930s customs house, its art deco interior preserved with meticulous care. Copenhagen's older jazz enthusiasts mingled with younger patrons, creating a comfortable anonymity.

Sam ordered a Carlsberg at the bar, scanning the room for potential contacts while appearing to admire the quintet on stage. His eyes caught on a tall, lanky man seated alone in the corner. Slender pianist's fingers tapped methodically against a tumbler of amber liquid. The face triggered recognition—from files, not personal encounter. Ivan Roshkov, Russian mathematician turned private security consultant. Last known position: cybersecurity director for a climate research coalition funded by Kessler Global Consulting.

Their eyes met briefly. Roshkov nodded once, then returned his attention to the stage. An invitation, not a threat. Yet.

Sam took his beer and crossed the room, sliding into the chair opposite Roshkov.

"The saxophone player misses every third grace note," Roshkov observed in perfect English, his accent barely detectable. "Fascinating how we notice patterns in imperfection more readily than in perfection."

"My father would disagree," Sam replied, establishing his cover. "He believes jazz exists in those imperfections."

Roshkov's pale blue eyes assessed him. "Ah, the American earth science teacher with a jazz musician father. You gave quite the presentation today on gathering climate data." He gestured toward the stage. "Perhaps there are imperfections in those patterns too."

"Weather follows natural laws," Sam countered, maintaining the academic persona. "Chaotic but ultimately predictable."

"Like human behavior." Roshkov smiled thinly. "Have you read much Dostoevsky, Professor Clayton?"

The question—seemingly off-topic—contained their first real exchange of information. Dostoevsky: the recognition phrase Marcus had prepared him for.

"Crime and Punishment made an impression," Sam replied carefully. "Though I found The Brothers Karamazov more illuminating about human nature."

Roshkov nodded, satisfied. "Brothers indeed. So complex, their relationships. One brother a sensualist, one an intellectual, one a spiritual seeker. Yet connected by blood, by history." He leaned forward. "Have you visited our exhibition at the Bella Center? 'Climate Futures'—I believe it would interest an educator like yourself."

"I planned to see it tomorrow."

"Tonight would be better. The data visualization room closes for maintenance tomorrow morning. Technical upgrades." Roshkov's fingers ceased their tapping. "Your Norwegian colleague—Magnussen—he found it most illuminating yesterday."

Sam kept his expression neutral despite the alarm bells. Anders hadn't mentioned visiting any exhibition.

"If you go," Roshkov continued, "notice the Arctic Ocean temperature projection. Something fascinating in the algorithm. A pattern within patterns." He stood abruptly. "Enjoy Copenhagen, Professor. The music continues between the notes."

The phrase—identical to one of Carmichael's favorite expressions—froze Sam momentarily. Roshkov couldn't possibly know that connection. Yet the words hung in the air as the Russian departed, leaving Sam alone with his half-finished beer and a decision.

Forty minutes later, Sam approached the Bella Center convention complex. The sprawling glass structure stood dark except for security lighting and a side entrance where a sign indicated "Climate Futures Exhibition - Open Until Midnight."

Inside, the exhibition hall stood nearly empty. Interactive displays illustrated rising sea levels, changing weather patterns, and global carbon emissions through elegant data visualizations. Only two other visitors browsed the exhibits—a young couple holding hands, pausing occasionally to read placards.

Sam moved methodically through the space until he reached the data visualization room. Inside, wall-sized displays cycled through climate projections. He located the Arctic Ocean temperature exhibit and began examining the projected warming patterns.

At first glance, the data appeared standard—consistent with accepted climate science. But as he studied the visualization, he spotted the anomaly. The temperature baseline had been subtly altered, creating a projection that exaggerated warming in specific regions while minimizing it in others.

Similar to what Anders had described, but more sophisticated.

Sam pulled out his phone, ostensibly checking messages while activating a specialized scanning application. He moved closer to the display terminal, positioning his phone to access the system. Within seconds, the program identified an external data feed influencing the projections—not from scientific sources but from a private server.

The magnitude dawned on him. This wasn't just academic fraud or politically motivated science. The alterations created artificial pressure points—strategically manipulating climate data to predict resource scarcities where none would naturally occur.

Someone was positioning themselves to control water resources across three continents.

A soft beep indicated his phone had established connection with the terminal. Sam initiated the extraction protocol, copying the server access logs and data modification records. Sixty seconds. His pulse quickened as the progress bar crawled across the screen.

"Finding what you're looking for, Professor Clayton?"

Sam turned to find a security guard watching him, hand resting casually near his belt. Not a standard museum guard—wrong stance, wrong posture. Too aware of sightlines, exits.

"Just fascinated by the visualization technique," Sam replied easily, sliding his phone into his pocket as the download completed. "My students back in New York would love this approach."

The guard smiled without warmth. "The exhibition closes in ten minutes. Perhaps you'd like to see our special collection before departing? It's in the lower level."

A trap, poorly disguised. "Actually, I should head back to my hotel. Early presentation tomorrow."

The guard's hand moved slightly closer to what Sam now recognized as a concealed weapon. "I insist. The director would be disappointed if you missed it."

Sam nodded affably, buying seconds to assess options. "Lead the way."

The guard gestured toward a service corridor. As they walked, Sam noticed a second security figure falling in behind them. Not good. He needed separation, distraction.

"I left my conference materials at the Arctic display," Sam said suddenly. "Mind if I grab them?"

Without waiting for permission, he turned back toward the exhibition hall. The first guard reached for his arm, but Sam was already moving, his pace quickening as he rounded the corner. Behind him, he heard urgent whispers, then footsteps.

Sam didn't run—running attracted attention. Instead, he moved with purpose through the exhibition hall, past the young couple still examining displays, through the main entrance where he'd entered. Outside, he turned left, away from the main thoroughfare, calculating routes.

The footsteps behind him accelerated. Sam abandoned pretense and broke into a sprint, cutting through a construction area adjacent to the center. His pursuers followed, no longer concerned with maintaining cover. One shouted in Danish, then English: "Stop! Security!"

Sam vaulted a low barrier, entered a partially completed structure. Scaffolding and plastic sheeting created a maze of temporary corridors. He navigated by instinct, hearing the guards closing the gap.

A flash of memory from Carmichael's training: "Create distance through environmental advantage." Sam grabbed a section of scaffolding and pulled it down behind him, buying precious seconds as his pursuers navigated the obstacle.

Emerging on the far side of the construction site, Sam oriented himself, spotting the lights of a main boulevard two blocks away. Public spaces, witnesses, safety. He pushed forward through a narrow alley, calculating his route back to the Admiral Hotel.

A figure stepped from the shadows ahead, blocking his path. Not one of the guards from the exhibition—someone else. Broader, more substantial presence. The man said nothing, simply raised his hand to reveal a pistol with silencer attached.

Sam didn't hesitate. He charged directly at the man, years of defensive training overriding instinct. The unexpectedness of the frontal assault created a split-second advantage—the man fired, but the hasty shot went wide. Sam crashed into him, driving his knee upward while grasping the gun hand.

They struggled briefly before the weapon clattered to the ground. The man landed a solid blow to Sam's ribs, driving the air from his lungs. Sam countered with a sharp strike to the throat, buying himself space to retrieve the fallen pistol.

As his fingers closed around the weapon, footsteps pounded at the alley entrance. The exhibition guards had caught up. Sam didn't wait—he sprinted toward the boulevard, weapon concealed inside his jacket.

Behind him, confusion erupted. The man with the silenced pistol wasn't working with the exhibition security team. Different operators, different agendas.

Sam reached the boulevard, immediately dropping the pace to a casual walk despite the fire in his lungs. He hailed an approaching taxi, glancing back to see his pursuers hesitating at the edge of the crowded street.

"Admiral Hotel, please," he told the driver, fighting to control his breathing. As the taxi pulled away, Sam carefully ejected the pistol's magazine, removed the round from the chamber, and separated the components. He would dispose of them in different locations between the taxi and hotel.

The flash drive felt impossibly heavy in his pocket. Whatever data it contained had just proven valuable enough for someone to risk an operation on foreign soil, at an international conference. The question was: who? And how did they know he'd discovered the anomaly?

Something bigger was happening. The manipulated climate data, Anders' findings, Roshkov's cryptic warning—connected pieces of a puzzle he couldn't yet assemble.

"You've stirred a nest of hornets," Phoebe observed calmly the next morning, sipping tea in the hotel's breakfast room. At sixty-seven, his mother maintained the bearing of the history professor she had been for decades. Only the slight tension around her eyes betrayed concern. "Two different teams. Interesting."

"Roshkov knew I'd be targeted," Sam said quietly. "The question is whether he was warning me or setting me up."

"Both, possibly." Phoebe stirred her tea precisely three times—a habit from decades of tradecraft. "Have you transmitted the data?"

"Not yet. I'm not convinced we have secure channels. Someone knew I was accessing that terminal within minutes."

"Your Dr. Magnussen hasn't appeared for his presentation this morning."

Sam felt his stomach tighten. "Conference administration?"

"Informed that he was called away on family emergency."

"That's not good."

"No." Phoebe's gaze drifted across the breakfast room, cataloging faces. "You mentioned Roshkov used your father's phrase about music. That suggests knowledge beyond operational parameters."

"He's playing a deeper game," Sam agreed.

"Most Russians do." She placed her teacup down. "I'll make contact with our embassy assets. You focus on your teacher cover today—be enthusiastic, forgettably professional. We'll arrange extraction of the data tonight."

Sam nodded, recognizing her shift to operational planning. Despite their complicated history, Phoebe

MacReynolds remained one of the most efficient intelligence operatives he'd ever known. Her academic career had provided perfect cover during the Cold War—her specialty in Northern European history creating natural opportunities for work behind the Iron Curtain.

"Forty-two years old, and still I'm giving you instructions," she said with unexpected softness. "Your father would find that amusing."

"Carmichael has always appreciated irony," Sam replied, the tension breaking momentarily.

"Indeed." Phoebe's gaze hardened again. "Be careful today, Samuel. Whatever you've stumbled upon has significant resources behind it. The exhibition displays alone would require substantial funding and institutional credibility."

"Kessler Global Consulting," Sam said. "They're the primary sponsor of the climate research coalition Roshkov works for."

"Richard Kessler." Phoebe's expression darkened. "Former CIA Director under the previous administration. Interesting connection."

"Too early to draw conclusions."

"Perhaps." She stood, gathering her conference materials. "But patterns exist for those willing to see them. Your father taught you that through music. I taught you through history. Different approaches to the same truth."

As she departed, Sam remained at the table, contemplating the weight of the flash drive still in his pocket. Climate data manipulated to create artificial resource scarcities. A former CIA Director's consulting firm. Professional security teams with contradictory agendas. Roshkov's warning.

Pieces of a puzzle larger than he'd initially imagined.

Sam's afternoon presentation proceeded without incident. He delivered his prepared remarks on engaging students with climate science through local data collection, answered predictable questions, and maintained his cover as an enthusiastic earth science teacher from upstate New York. No one watching would connect him to the security incident at the Bella Center the previous night.

Throughout the day, he monitored the conference attendees for familiar faces from the exhibition. None appeared. Either they'd maintained better cover than he'd realized, or they'd withdrawn to reassess after last night's confrontation.

By evening, his planned rendezvous with Phoebe at a café near Nyhavn had been arranged. He would transfer the data, and she would ensure it reached Marcus through diplomatic channels. Sam had just packed his presentation materials when his phone vibrated with a text message.

Unknown number: "Meeting compromised. New location: Christiansborg Palace garden, north entrance, 20:00."

The message followed proper emergency protocols, but something felt wrong. The palace gardens offered too many approach vectors, too little protective cover. Sam sent the confirmation response as required, then added coded language indicating he would need verification on site.

He checked his watch—18:45. If the meeting had been compromised, he needed a secure location to assess the data before the rendezvous. His hotel room wasn't safe. Instead, he made his way to a 24-hour internet café five blocks from his hotel, far from the conference venues.

Inside, Sam purchased an hour of computer time and selected a workstation with clear sightlines to both entrance and emergency exit. He inserted the flash drive, using specialized software to examine its contents without opening files directly.

What he found confirmed his suspicions. The climate data alterations weren't random—they followed carefully designed parameters, creating false projections of drought conditions in regions with stable water sources while minimizing concerns in actually vulnerable areas.

A map emerged from the manipulated data points—strategic resource control across Northern Africa, Central Asia, and parts of South America. Regions where water rights could be quietly acquired based on artificially pessimistic climate projections, then leveraged for tremendous profit when the actual conditions proved better than forecast.

But the data contained something else—user access logs showing connections to servers operated by a constellation of research institutes, all with funding ties to Kessler Global Consulting. And one name appearing repeatedly in the authorization codes: RK001.

Richard Kessler himself.

Sam copied the essential data to a secure cloud server using encryption protocols only Marcus could access. Insurance, in case tonight's meeting went wrong. He removed the flash drive, prepared to head toward Christiansborg Palace, when movement at the café entrance caught his attention.

Two men entered, scanning the room with practiced efficiency. Different from last night's pursuers, but same professional demeanor. One spoke briefly to the café attendant, who pointed in Sam's direction.

No time for subtlety. Sam closed his session and moved toward the emergency exit, activating the protocol he'd established with Phoebe for abort scenarios. His phone would now broadcast a distress signal while appearing powered down.

Outside, light rain had begun falling, slicking the cobblestones and reducing visibility—both advantage and handicap. Sam moved quickly through back streets, adjusting his route toward the palace gardens while watching for surveillance. If the meeting location had been compromised, then someone had intercepted communications between him and Phoebe—a concerning development.

When he reached the palace perimeter, Sam circled the entire complex once, identifying multiple surveillance teams positioned around the north entrance. His mother wasn't visible, and the pattern of operatives suggested an ambush rather than a security detail.

Sam altered course, heading instead toward their emergency fallback—the Copenhagen Public Library. If Phoebe had recognized the same threat, she would meet him there, at the Norse mythology section, per established protocol.

The library stood quiet at this hour, only a handful of patrons browsing among the modernist interior. Sam moved casually through the stacks until he reached the designated area, scanning for his mother's distinctive profile.

Empty.

He waited precisely seven minutes—their agreed timing—before accepting that Phoebe wasn't coming. Either she'd been detained or she'd identified a threat and activated her own contingency plan. Either way, his priority now was securing the data and extracting himself from Copenhagen.

As Sam turned to leave, a library assistant approached, carrying a stack of books for reshelving.

"Excuse me, sir," she said in accented English. "I believe you dropped this." She held out a folded Danish newspaper.

Sam hadn't been carrying anything, but he recognized the approach. "Thank you. I've been looking for today's crossword."

Taking the newspaper, he tucked it under his arm and exited the library, walking three blocks before finding a quiet doorway to examine the delivery. Inside the folded paper, he found a handwritten note in Phoebe's precise script:

"Baltic Queen ferry. Midnight departure to Stockholm. Cabin 307. Contact compromised. Trust no established channels."

Below that, another line in different handwriting:

"The music continues between the notes. Remember Copenhagen pattern when water rises. -R"

Roshkov. The Russian had somehow intercepted their emergency protocols or coordinated with

Phoebe directly. Either possibility raised troubling questions.

Sam checked his watch—21:38. Less than two and a half hours to reach the ferry terminal, acquire a ticket, and board without being intercepted. He disposed of the newspaper and note, then began navigating toward the harbor, maintaining counter-surveillance measures despite the worsening weather.

The Baltic Queen loomed at the terminal, its massive white hull illuminated against the night sky. Sam had purchased a ticket using cash and emergency credentials, then boarded among a group of late-arriving passengers. Now, standing at the ship's rail as departure preparations continued, he watched the terminal for signs of pursuit.

Multiple figures moved with purpose through the embarkation area, some in plain clothes, others in security uniforms. Searching. Copenhagen police had been activated, either through legitimate channels or compromised ones.

The ship's horn sounded, announcing imminent departure. Sam remained at the rail until the gangway retracted and the vessel began pulling away from the dock. Only then did he move toward the passenger cabins, locating 307 and knocking softly.

Phoebe opened the door, ushering him inside quickly. She had changed her appearance—hair now darker and pulled back, clothing different from her conference attire.

"You've been shot," she said immediately, gesturing to his sleeve where a dark stain had spread.

Sam looked down in surprise. During his evasion route, he'd scraped against a metal fence. What he'd dismissed as a minor cut now revealed itself as a bullet graze—likely from the café confrontation.

"Superficial," he assessed, though the adrenaline fade made the wound throb uncomfortably. "What happened at the rendezvous?"

"Intercepted communications." Phoebe moved to the cabin's small bathroom, returning with a first aid kit. "Someone has compromised our standard protocols. I never sent the text redirecting you to the palace gardens."

Sam allowed her to clean and bandage the wound while processing the implications. "How did you know to leave the message at the library?"

"I didn't. I went there as per our contingency, but you'd already left. I left the note with the librarian I've worked with before."

"Then who gave her the note to pass to me?"

Phoebe's hands paused in their methodical wrapping. "What do you mean?"

"There was a second message. From Roshkov."

Her expression hardened. "What did it say?"

Sam repeated the cryptic line about music and water.

"Curious." Phoebe secured the bandage. "Either he's playing an elaborate game, or—"

"He's trying to help," Sam finished. "But why?"

"Russians rarely act from simple motivations." She disposed of the bloodied cotton pads. "Did you secure the data?"

"Uploaded to the emergency server. But if our communications are compromised—"

"We adapt." Phoebe's voice carried the authority of decades in field operations. "Stockholm first. Then separate routes home. No electronic communications, no standard protocols."

Sam nodded, feeling the weight of what they'd stumbled upon. "The data shows systematic manipulation of climate projections to create artificial water scarcities—for profit. And it connects directly to Richard Kessler."

"The former CIA Director using his climate security firm to manipulate global resources." Phoebe shook her head. "Bold, even for him."

"And just the beginning, I think." Sam moved to the cabin window, watching Copenhagen's lights recede into the distance. "What happened to Anders Magnussen? The Norwegian climatologist?"

"Unknown. His hotel room was cleared out. No trace in conference records."

The implication hung between them. Anders had noticed the same data anomalies, had directed Sam to The Standard where Roshkov made contact. Now he had vanished.

"We've discovered something significant," Phoebe said finally. "Something worth killing for."

"Or worth sacrificing a respected scientist for," Sam agreed grimly. "The question is, how deep does this go? And who can we trust to help stop it?"

The ferry's engines rumbled beneath them as the Baltic Queen entered open water, carrying them away from Copenhagen and the first fragments of a conspiracy that seemed to reach into the highest levels of global power.

Sam touched the flash drive in his pocket, now empty but still evidence of what he'd discovered. Climate data weaponized for resource control—a concept so audacious it would sound paranoid if described. Yet the evidence existed, transmitted to Marcus through channels hopefully still secure.

The stakes had suddenly expanded far beyond what Sam had anticipated when arriving for a teachers' conference. Whatever he'd stumbled upon in Copenhagen's dark October night would follow him home to Plattsburgh, to his classroom, to his family.

To Danielle, Ellie and little Rae, and Cade—just three years old—waiting at home, unaware of the shadow that had just fallen across their future.

The ferry pushed onward through the darkness, carrying them toward Stockholm and the long journey home—away from Copenhagen but toward a confrontation years in the making.

Chapter 2
East Coast Trek
July-August 2011

Sunrise painted the highway in golden hues as Sam Clayton adjusted the rearview mirror of the black Suburban. His gaze swept across his sleeping family – Danielle reclined in the passenger seat, nine-year-old Ellie and seven-year-old Rae sharing earbuds in the middle row, four-year-old Cade absorbed in his picture book, and one-year-old Mackie finally dozing in his car seat after fussing through Newark.

Sam allowed himself a moment of contentment. This was the life he'd built – the one that felt most real. Teacher, husband, father. The other life remained carefully compartmentalized, tucked away during family vacations like this East Coast trek they'd spent months planning.

Until the events following Copenhagen had changed everything.

"You're thinking too loud," Danielle murmured, eyes still closed. She reached across the console and squeezed his hand. "We're almost there, right?"

"Twenty minutes to the hotel in Cherry Hill," Sam confirmed, checking the GPS. "You should see the itinerary Ellie made. Every monument and museum perfectly scheduled with travel time between."

Danielle smiled, eyes still closed. "Wonder where she gets that from."

The irony wasn't lost on Sam. His daughter's meticulous planning mirrored his own operational preparations – though Ellie's schedule centered around the National Air and Space Museum rather than dead drops at historical monuments.

"Dad, is that the Philadelphia skyline?" Ellie pressed her face against the window, suddenly alert.

"Close, but we're still seeing Camden. Philadelphia's across the river." Sam pointed toward the hazy skyline emerging through morning mist. "We'll head there tomorrow after breakfast."

"At IHOP," Cade insisted, looking up from his book. "You promised pancakes with faces."

"I remember, buddy." Sam tousled his son's hair, catching Danielle's knowing look. Four-year-old Cade's memory for details was already remarkably precise.

As Sam navigated the final miles to their hotel, his mind kept returning to Marcus Cartier's encrypted message delivered just before they'd left Plattsburgh: "Eastern assets requiring verification. Opportunity in travels. Usual protocols."

The message had been clear. Their family vacation would become operational cover.

The Liberty Bell gleamed dully under museum lights as tourists circled the iconic American symbol. Sam kept one hand on Cade's shoulder while surveying the crowded exhibition space. His gaze lingered on a man sketching the bell in a small notebook – the third time they'd crossed paths that morning.

"Dad, did you know the Liberty Bell weighs over 2,000 pounds?" Ellie recited from her guidebook. "And the crack was from the first time they rang it?"

"Actually," Sam corrected gently, "that's a common misconception. The original crack was repaired, but it cracked again decades later. The large crack we see now came from an attempt to repair the bell for George Washington's birthday in 1846."

"How do you know that?" Rae asked, impressed.

"I read," Sam replied with a wink, spotting Danielle returning with Mackie from a diaper change.

"Did Daddy give another history lesson?" Danielle asked, shifting Mackie to her other hip.

"He knows everything," Cade declared with absolute certainty.

"Not everything, buddy," Sam said, making a mental note of the man with the sketchbook leaving precisely on schedule. "Just some things."

They moved through the exhibit as Sam's attention divided between his family's experience and the subtle operational awareness that had become second nature. The crowds provided perfect cover as he paused at a specific display case, ostensibly reading about the bell's dimensions while his hand brushed against the underside of the informational plaque.

His fingers detected the small data chip secured with putty – exactly where it was supposed to be.

"Daddy, I'm hungry," Cade announced, tugging Sam's hand and inadvertently providing the perfect distraction as Sam palmed the chip and slipped it into his pocket.

"Me too, little man," Sam agreed, checking his watch. "Perfect timing for lunch before we see Independence Hall. Who wants cheesesteaks?"

As they exited into the Philadelphia summer heat, Sam cast one final glance behind them. The exchange had been smooth – no one watching, nothing to suggest this family vacation doubled as something else entirely.

The National Mall stretched before them like an enormous green carpet, Washington Monument piercing the cerulean sky. Sam wiped sweat from his brow as he pushed Mackie's stroller across the sunbaked pathways of the nation's capital. July in D.C. was punishingly hot, the humidity creating a visible haze over the city.

"Can we go to the Air and Space Museum next?" Ellie asked, consulting her meticulous itinerary. "We have reservations for the planetarium show at 2:30."

"Actually," Danielle interjected, fanning herself with a museum map, "I think we need to find somewhere air-conditioned for lunch first. This heat is brutal."

"The Smithsonian cafeteria has incredible chicken fingers," Sam suggested, silently calculating the time needed to reach his next checkpoint. "And it's right on the way."

They made their way toward the museum complex, joining streams of tourists seeking refuge from the heat. Sam maintained casual awareness of their surroundings – a habit impossible to break even during family time. Three days in Washington had allowed him to complete two data exchanges while maintaining the appearance of an ordinary family vacation.

Inside the cafeteria, blessed air conditioning washed over them as Sam secured a table while Danielle took the children to select their lunch. He used the moment alone to transfer the data chip from Philadelphia into a specially modified phone, initiating the encrypted upload while appearing to check his email.

"Daddy, they have dinosaur-shaped chicken nuggets!" Cade announced triumphantly, returning with Danielle and balancing his tray with careful concentration.

"Outstanding choice, paleontologist Clayton," Sam replied, pocketing his phone as the upload completed.

Lunch passed with excited chatter about aircraft and space shuttles until Mackie began fussing in his high chair, overtired from the morning's activities.

"I can take him outside for a bit," Sam offered. "He might nap in the stroller."

"I want to go with Dad," Cade declared, abandoning his half-eaten lunch.

Danielle nodded. "We'll meet you in the main hall in fifteen minutes? The girls want to see the Wright Brothers exhibit before the planetarium show."

Outside, Sam pushed the stroller with one hand and held Cade's with the other, meandering toward a less crowded area where Mackie might settle. The boy was already heavy-lidded, thumb in mouth as the stroller's motion worked its magic.

"Dad, can we see the moon rocks?" Cade asked, skipping alongside him.

"Absolutely. As soon as Mackie—" Sam's words caught as he detected the subtle shift in the crowd around them. Two men in baseball caps had appeared on either side of the pathway, moving with too much purpose among the meandering tourists.

Sam's training kicked in immediately as he scanned for additional threats. There – a third man by the information kiosk, speaking into his sleeve.

"Cade," Sam said, keeping his voice calm while tightening his grip on his son's hand. "Let's play a game. We're going to walk very fast back to the museum, okay?"

Cade looked up, his expressive face registering confusion. "Why?"

"Because it's a race," Sam improvised, already turning the stroller. "Let's see how quickly we can find Mom and your sisters."

They had covered perhaps ten yards when the first man accelerated, cutting diagonally to intercept their path. Sam's heartbeat remained steady even as adrenaline flooded his system. The man was reaching inside his jacket – not for a weapon, Sam assessed, but likely for credentials.

Not law enforcement, Sam was certain. The coordination was too informal, the positions too amateur. Which meant something far worse.

"Actually, buddy, new plan," Sam said, lifting Cade onto his hip while maintaining his grip on the stroller. "We're going to run."

Sam pushed through a family of tourists, creating momentary confusion as he changed direction toward a museum service entrance he'd noted earlier. Years of training had taught him to always locate exits, alternative routes, potential safe zones.

"Dad?" Cade's voice wavered with uncertainty.

"Just hang on tight," Sam instructed, increasing his pace without breaking into an obvious run that would attract attention.

He could hear footsteps following, voices speaking into communications devices. The service entrance loomed ahead – likely locked, but worth trying. As they approached, the door suddenly opened as a maintenance worker emerged, providing the perfect opportunity.

"Excuse us," Sam said pleasantly, brushing past the startled employee. "My son needs the restroom urgently."

Inside the service corridor, Sam moved swiftly, Cade clinging to his neck while Mackie, disturbed by the sudden movement, began crying in the stroller. Sam located a staff elevator, jabbing the call button repeatedly.

"It's okay, buddy," he reassured Cade, whose wide eyes reflected growing fear. "We're playing hide and seek. Those men are 'it' and we don't want to be caught, right?"

Cade nodded solemnly, old enough to sense something was wrong but young enough to accept the game explanation.

The elevator arrived with a cheerful ding. Sam maneuvered the stroller inside, pressing the button for the main exhibition level where Danielle and the girls would be waiting. As the doors closed, he caught a glimpse of one of the men entering the service corridor.

Reaching into his pocket, Sam retrieved his phone and sent a pre-programmed text to Danielle: TURTLE. This emergency code, established after his return from Copenhagen two years ago when he'd insisted on basic family security measures, indicated potential threat, proceed to predetermined safe location.

The elevator opened onto the bustling main hall. Sam scanned the crowd, spotting Danielle and the girls precisely where they'd agreed to meet. Her expression shifted instantly upon seeing them, concern flashing across her face as she saw Cade clutched protectively in Sam's arms, then confusion as she checked her phone.

"Sam?" she questioned, voice rising with concern. "What's going on?"

"We need to leave. Now," he replied, voice low but urgent.

"But the planetarium—" Ellie began to protest.

"Change of plans, girls," Danielle said, studying Sam's face with growing alarm. "Something's happened. We're heading back to the hotel."

"Dad, what happened to our game?" Cade asked, still thinking they were playing hide and seek.

Sam glanced around, spotting one of the men entering the far side of the hall. "The game's not over, buddy. We need to get back to home base without being tagged."

Danielle's alarmed gaze followed Sam's. "Sam, who are those men? What's happening?"

"I'll explain at the hotel," he whispered, guiding them toward a side exit. "Right now, we need to move."

"What? Why?" Danielle whispered as they moved through the crowd, "You're scaring me."

"I know," Sam acknowledged, leading them through the exit. "But I need you to follow my lead right now."

As they exited onto a less crowded side street, Danielle's face had paled. Sam flagged down a taxi while maintaining surveillance of their surroundings.

"What? Who would be interested in a four-year-old boy? Was it security? Police?" Danielle asked as they moved toward the cab, struggling to make sense of the situation.

The questions hung between them as Sam helped his family into the vehicle, giving the driver their hotel address.

"I don't know yet," Sam admitted, holding her gaze. "But I intend to find out."

The hotel room door closed with a solid click as Sam engaged the security lock and privacy bolt. He methodically checked the windows, drew the curtains, and swept the room visually before speaking.

Danielle stood rigidly in the center of the room, arms crossed tightly across her chest, watching these unfamiliar movements with growing unease. The older children were settled in the adjoining room with cartoons, Mackie finally asleep in the portable crib.

"Okay," she said, voice trembling with a mixture of fear and anger. "The kids are safe. Now tell me what the hell is going on."

Sam turned to face her, and for the first time in their marriage, Danielle saw uncertainty in his eyes—as though he'd rehearsed every scenario except this one.

"I don't even know where to begin," he said quietly.

"How about with who you really are?" Danielle's voice cracked. "Because the man I saw today— calculating escape routes, evading pursuers, sending coded messages—that's not the high school science teacher I married."

Sam sank onto the edge of the bed. "I am a teacher, Danielle. That's not a lie. But I'm also... something else."

"Nine years," she whispered, tears welling. "Nine years of marriage, four children together, and there's a 'something else' you never thought to mention?"

"I couldn't tell you. I was protecting you—"

"Don't," Danielle cut him off, holding up a hand. "Don't you dare say you were protecting me by lying to me every single day of our marriage."

"Not every day," Sam insisted. "Most days, I'm exactly who you think I am."

"Except when you're not." Danielle paced the small room, hands shaking. "God, Sam. Who were those men? What did they want with Cade? With our son?"

Sam's hesitation only fueled her panic.

"Tell me!" she demanded, her voice rising before she caught herself, glancing toward the connecting door. "Our children are in danger, and I don't even know why."

"I work with an intelligence organization," Sam finally admitted. "Not officially with any government, but... adjacent. We monitor certain activities, gather information."

Danielle stared at him as though seeing a stranger. "You're a spy? Is that what you're telling me?"

"That's... simplistic, but close enough."

"And what does this have to do with our four-year-old?" The tremor in her voice had been replaced by steel.

"I don't know yet," Sam said. "But those men today were specifically tracking Cade, not me. Not Mackie. Just Cade."

"Why would anyone target a child?" Danielle's scientific mind fought to make sense of the impossible.

"I need to contact my... colleague," Sam said carefully. "He might have answers."

"Your handler, you mean," Danielle corrected bitterly. "Like in the movies."

Sam didn't deny it as he retrieved a laptop she'd never seen before from a compartment in his luggage she hadn't known existed. The casual efficiency with which he accessed hidden panels and set up equipment only underscored how completely she'd been deceived.

"How many other secrets are there, Sam?" she asked quietly. "Is Samuel Clayton even your real name?"

"Yes," he assured her quickly. "Everything about our life together is real, Danielle. My feelings for you, for our children—that's all real."

"Just with a side of espionage," she said flatly, watching him establish what he explained was a secure connection.

As Sam began typing, Danielle retreated to the bathroom, closing the door behind her. Only then did she allow the tears to fall, pressing her hand against her mouth to muffle the sound. Her mind raced through years of memories, recontextualizing them, questioning which moments had been genuine and which had been cover.

The research trips. The conferences. The late-night phone calls. How many had been for his other life?

When she emerged minutes later, face washed and composure somewhat restored, Sam was staring at his screen, expression grim.

"What is it?" she asked, maternal instinct overriding her personal turmoil.

"We're being watched," Sam said quietly. "Not just today. For years. Since Copenhagen."

"Since Copenhagen?" Danielle repeated. "Your teachers' conference two years ago?"

Sam nodded. "It wasn't exactly a teachers' conference."

"Of course it wasn't," Danielle said bitterly. "What was it really? No, wait—can you even tell me, or is that classified too?"

"I can tell you some of it," Sam said. "I should have told you after it happened."

"Why didn't you?" The hurt in her voice was palpable.

"Training," Sam admitted. "Decades of compartmentalization. Keeping my worlds separate was second nature."

"Well, your worlds have collided now," Danielle said. "And our children are caught in the middle."

Sam turned the laptop toward her, showing a message on screen: Maintain cover. Proceed to Raleigh as planned. Additional security measures incoming. Compromised asset in custody reveals wider surveillance than previously known. All packages monitored.

"Packages?" Danielle questioned. "You mean our children?"

Sam nodded gravely. "They're watching all of them. Not just Cade."

The maternal fury that rose in Danielle's chest surprised even her with its intensity. "Who is 'they'? And why are they watching our children?"

"That's what we need to find out," Sam said.

"We?" Danielle's laugh was brittle. "Suddenly I'm part of the team?"

"Danielle, I know this is a lot—"

"A lot?" she interrupted. "Sam, you've just told me our entire life is a lie and someone is targeting our children. 'A lot' doesn't begin to cover it."

She sank into the chair opposite him, the weight of the situation momentarily overwhelming her anger. "I don't even know if I can trust you anymore."

"You can," Sam said firmly. "In this, if nothing else—I will do anything to protect our family."

Danielle studied his face, searching for the husband she thought she knew. "What happens now?"

"We need to get somewhere secure," Sam explained. "Somewhere with support systems in place."

"Raleigh," Danielle realized. "Flynn is part of this too, isn't he?"

Sam's silence was answer enough.

"My God. Does Melissa know? Am I the only one who's been kept in the dark all these years?"

"Melissa has... limited awareness," Sam admitted. "For her protection."

"Limited awareness," Danielle repeated. "So she knows more than I did. That's just... perfect."

She stood abruptly. "I need to check on the children."

"Danielle," Sam called softly as she moved toward the connecting door. "I need to know... are you with me on this? Not for my sake, but for theirs?"

She paused, her back to him, shoulders rigid with tension. When she turned, her face was set with determination despite the tear tracks still visible.

"I'm with them," she clarified. "Our children. I'll do whatever it takes to keep them safe, even if that means working with you right now. But don't mistake that for forgiveness, Sam. Or trust."

The words stung, but Sam nodded, accepting this conditional alliance. "That's fair."

"And when this is over," Danielle continued, "when our children are safe, we are going to have a very long conversation about what happens next. For all of us."

"I understand," Sam agreed quietly.

Danielle hesitated at the door. "I need to pull myself together before I see them. They can't know something's wrong."

"I've always admired your strength," Sam said softly.

"Don't," Danielle cut him off. "Don't compliment me right now. I don't even know who you're seeing when you look at me."

With that, she disappeared into the adjoining room, leaving Sam alone with the weight of his divided life finally crashing down around him.

"Everyone has their sunscreen?" Danielle asked, her voice impressively normal as she helped Mackie with his float in the hotel pool. Only Sam could detect the strain beneath her carefully composed exterior.

Six hours had passed since their confrontation in the hotel room. Six hours of Danielle processing the unthinkable while maintaining a calm façade for their children. She'd retreated to the bathroom twice more to compose herself in private, and Sam had caught her staring at him with wounded, questioning eyes whenever the children weren't looking.

"Mom, can I get a popsicle from the snack bar?" Rae asked, pointing to the small kiosk.

"In a little while, honey," Danielle replied, her gaze subtly tracking each person who entered the pool area. Another new behavior—hypervigilance—that broke Sam's heart to witness.

Right on schedule, a man in blue swim trunks and a Syracuse University cap entered the pool area, carrying a rolled towel under his arm. He selected a lounge chair two removed from Sam's position.

Sam caught Danielle's eye, giving a nearly imperceptible nod toward the man. Her eyes widened slightly before her scientific mind visibly processed the information, making connections.

"I think I'll get those popsicles now," Sam announced, standing and stretching casually. "Anyone want anything specific?"

After collecting requests, Sam walked past the courier, who appeared to be applying sunscreen. Their eyes never met, but as Sam passed, the man placed his towel on the neighboring chair—the rolled end containing the concealed package pointing toward Sam's belongings.

Sam completed his circuit to the snack bar, returning with treats for everyone. As he distributed them, he casually collected his own towel, simultaneously retrieving the small package from the courier's towel.

Danielle watched the exchange, her face carefully neutral save for a slight tightening around her eyes. The ease with which Sam conducted this operation— in full view of dozens of people, without drawing any attention—unsettled her deeply. How many other exchanges had he conducted right under her nose over the years?

"Daddy, watch me swim underwater!" Cade called out.

"I'm watching, buddy," Sam replied, settling back into his chair as the courier departed.

"Cade, don't go too deep," Danielle cautioned, her protective instincts heightened to new levels. She moved closer to Sam, pretending to apply more sunscreen.

"That was a dead drop, wasn't it?" she whispered, the espionage terminology sounding foreign on her lips. "Like in the movies."

"Something like that," Sam conceded.

"And that man—was he one of yours or theirs?"

"Ours," Sam assured her. "He's bringing information that might help us understand what's happening."

Danielle glanced at their children playing in the water, her expression hardening. "This isn't a movie, Sam. This is our life. Our children's lives."

"I know," he said quietly.

"When can you look at... whatever that is?" She nodded toward the concealed package.

"Tonight. After they're asleep."

Danielle nodded, standing abruptly. "I'm going to swim with the kids. At least one of us should be having an honest interaction with them today."

The barb landed as intended, and Sam accepted it without protest. He watched as Danielle dove gracefully into the pool, surfacing with a forced smile as Ellie swam toward her. His wife was adapting to this new reality with remarkable speed —channeling her anger and fear into protective action.

He only hoped she could eventually find room for forgiveness alongside that formidable strength.

The shower ran in the background, masking their voices as Sam opened the package in the hotel bathroom. Danielle stood with arms crossed, maintaining physical distance between them even in the confined space.

Sam withdrew a small device resembling a standard USB drive and a note with a single sentence: Subject located within Smithsonian security. Access to family surveillance maintained since October 2009.

"October 2009," Danielle read over his shoulder. "Copenhagen."

"Yes," Sam confirmed, bracing himself for her reaction.

The final item in the package silenced any response she might have made—a small stack of surveillance photographs. Their children at school in Plattsburgh. Danielle shopping at the farmers' market. Cade playing soccer in their backyard.

"Oh my God," Danielle whispered, snatching the photos and rifling through them with increasing horror. "They've been watching us? In our home? At their schools?"

The last photograph showed Cade solving a complex puzzle designed for children twice his age, the timestamp indicating it had been taken just three weeks earlier.

"How could you let this happen?" Danielle demanded, voice rising despite the running water. "How could you bring this into our lives?"

"I didn't know," Sam insisted, his own shock evident. "I had no idea they were watching the children. Watching you."

"But you knew there was a 'they' to worry about," Danielle countered, tears threatening again. "You knew there were people who might target your family, and you said nothing. Did nothing."

"I did do something," Sam argued. "The security system at the house, the cameras, the protocols—"

"The mysterious 'home improvements' last year," Danielle realized. "The new alarm system. You weren't being paranoid about break-ins at all."

Sam shook his head, watching as his wife processed years of deception in real time.

"They're watching the children," Sam whispered, a chill running through him despite the steam-filled bathroom.

Danielle clutched the photographs to her chest, maternal fury replacing shock. "We're leaving. Tonight."

"We can't," Sam countered. "Not without drawing attention. We need to maintain cover, make it look normal."

"Normal?" Danielle's voice cracked. "There is no normal anymore, Sam. Not after this."

"First light," Sam suggested instead. "We'll leave at first light, tell the kids something came up."

Danielle nodded sharply, the scientist in her recognizing the tactical necessity despite her emotional turmoil. "A family matter in Raleigh. We'll emphasize visiting Flynn and Melissa, maybe see Mom in Winston-Salem while we're there."

Sam nodded, surprised at how quickly she'd pivoted to operational thinking. "Flynn and Melissa's place is our best safe location."

"And after that?" Danielle asked. "What happens when our children are safe? To us?"

The question hung between them, loaded with implications Sam couldn't begin to address.

"One crisis at a time," he said softly.

Danielle studied him for a long moment, her eyes revealing a complex mix of hurt, anger, and something else—a fierce determination that Sam recognized from her years of scientific research.

"These people," she said, tapping the photographs, "whoever they are. They're targeting our son. Our four-year-old boy."

"Yes."

"Then they've made a critical mistake," Danielle said, her voice deadly calm. "Because nothing on earth is more dangerous than a mother protecting her children."

Sam recognized the shift in that moment—Danielle moving from betrayed wife to protective mother, finding purpose in the chaos. It didn't erase the damage to their marriage, but it created a foundation for cooperation that transcended personal hurt.

"We'll protect them," Sam promised. "Together."

"Not together," Danielle corrected, handing the photographs back to him. "Alongside each other. There's a difference."

That night, as Danielle finally drifted to sleep beside him, maintaining a careful distance even in slumber, Sam stared at the ceiling, hyperaware of every sound in the hotel corridor. The worlds he'd kept so carefully separated - family man and intelligence operative - were colliding in the worst possible way.

His children were being watched. Assessed. For what purpose, he couldn't yet determine - but the implication was clear. Someone believed Cade had inherited something valuable from his father. Something worth monitoring.

Something worth taking.

Departure procedures went smoothly with a fabricated story about a family matter requiring their attention in Raleigh. The adjusted itinerary emphasized visiting Flynn and Melissa, plus the opportunity to see Danielle's mother in nearby Winston-Salem, before returning to Plattsburgh. The children had accepted the explanation with minimal disappointment after promises that they'd still make special stops along the route.

"We're still going to Aunt Melissa's, right?" Rae asked from the middle row as their Suburban joined morning traffic heading south from Washington.

"Absolutely," Sam confirmed, eyes constantly checking mirrors for surveillance. "We'll spend a couple days with them in Raleigh, then head home."

"And we'll see Grandma in Winston-Salem too?" Rae asked hopefully.

"Yes," Danielle confirmed. "We'll drive over for a day trip while we're staying with Aunt Melissa and Uncle Flynn."

Since leaving the hotel, Sam had employed every counter-surveillance tactic possible while maintaining the appearance of normal family travel. Their route included unexpected turns, brief stops at crowded rest areas with multiple exits, and passing through areas where video surveillance could be identified and avoided.

By mid-afternoon, Sam was reasonably confident they'd shed any physical tail. The digital monitoring was another matter – one that would require Marcus Cartier's resources to resolve.

"Dinosaur book, please," Cade requested from his car seat, reaching toward his backpack just beyond his grasp.

Ellie retrieved it for him, then returned to her travel journal. "Dad, can we still stop at Hershey's on the way home? You promised we could make our own chocolate bars."

"We'll try, sweetheart," Sam answered, meeting Danielle's eyes briefly. Their silent communication had always been effective, but in the past twenty-four hours it had evolved into something deeper – partnership in protection, if not in marriage.

They reached Raleigh by evening, the familiar surroundings of Melissa and Flynn's neighborhood providing the first real sense of security since the incident. Flynn Evans, Danielle's brother-in-law, greeted them in the driveway with characteristic enthusiasm that didn't quite mask his operational awareness.

"Long drive today," he observed, helping unload luggage. "Kids must be exhausted."

"Swimming pool time!" Melissa announced, emerging from the house to embrace her sister. "Your cousins are already waiting for you."

As the children raced inside, Flynn's expression shifted subtly. "Everything secure?" he asked quietly.

"Controlled compromise," Sam replied in the same low tone. "Need comms tonight."

Flynn nodded once. "Office is prepped. After dinner."

Danielle watched this exchange with new understanding, no longer excluded from the operational language that had once been Sam's separate world. Her eyes narrowed at Melissa, clearly wondering how much her sister knew.

Dinner passed with the joyful chaos of cousins reunited, Melissa's fifteen-year-old Alexander and eleven-year-old James entertaining their younger cousins with video games and stories. Sam observed Cade's interaction with his cousins closely, noting how his son's quiet intelligence manifested in solving cooperative game challenges.

Later, after the children were settled with a movie in the basement media room, Sam and Flynn retreated to the home office. Danielle followed, her expression making it clear this wasn't optional.

"Sam, I need to know what's happening," she insisted. "Those men tried to take our son."

Flynn raised an eyebrow at Sam, who hesitated before nodding. "She deserves to know some of this. Not everything, but enough."

The office transformed with the press of a hidden switch, computer monitors descending from ceiling compartments as Flynn activated specialized equipment concealed within ordinary furniture. Within minutes, they had established a secure connection to Marcus.

"Verify your status," Marcus's voice came through, deliberately distorted by security protocols.

"Family secure at checkpoint Raleigh," Sam responded. "Surveillance indicated specific interest in C-package. Photographs recovered from courier show monitoring since Copenhagen, with particular focus on cognitive capabilities."

A moment of silence followed before Marcus continued. "Analysis of captured operative's materials confirms our suspicions. The Consortium has identified potential in the next generation. Your activation was not coincidental, Samuel."

Sam felt Danielle stiffen beside him, trying to piece together the fragments of information. He turned to her, explaining in simplified terms, "After my trip to Copenhagen, certain people became interested in our family. They recognized patterns of thinking, problem-solving abilities."

"In our children?" Danielle whispered, understanding dawning. "They're watching our children? Because of puzzles and games?"

Sam nodded, turning back to the communication. "Marcus, Danielle needs to understand the basics. These are her children too."

"Limited information is acceptable given the circumstances," Marcus replied after a pause. "Explain that certain capabilities appear to be inherited. The Consortium recognized unique perspectives that could be valuable to them. They've been monitoring families with similar capabilities."

Danielle's voice held controlled outrage as she processed this. "They're watching children? For what purpose?"

"Not just watching," Flynn interjected, bringing up a document on the main screen. "Assessing. Recruiting, potentially."

Sam studied the document – personnel files for a specialized program targeting gifted children with specific cognitive traits. Most disturbing was a section clearly labeled "Acquisition Protocols."

"They tried to take him," Sam said flatly. "At the Smithsonian."

"Assessment only, we believe," Marcus responded. "But yes, the potential for acquisition exists. Your counter-measures were appropriate."

"They're four, seven, and nine years old," Danielle stated, her scientist's precision carrying through even in anger. "You can't possibly expect them to be involved in whatever this is."

"Not involved," Marcus clarified. "Protected. The operational awareness you've shown since this began, Danielle, suggests you understand the necessity."

Sam watched his wife absorb this, seeing the same calculation in her eyes that he recognized in himself – weighing risk, considering variables, prioritizing safety.

"What's our next move?" Sam asked.

"Complete your vacation as adjusted," Marcus instructed. "Maintain family normalcy. Upon return, enhanced security protocols will be implemented for your residence and the children's activities. We'll establish regular check-ins through Flynn's channels."

When the conversation turned to specific operational details, Flynn gently suggested Danielle might want to check on the children. Though clearly reluctant, she understood this was as far as her inclusion would extend today.

"This isn't over," she told Sam quietly before leaving. "They're our children. I need to know how to protect them."

After she left, the conversation continued with specific security recommendations, but Sam's mind kept returning to the photographs. His children – their talents, their potential – had been noticed by people willing to "acquire" them for unknown purposes.

The meeting concluded with Flynn providing specialized equipment disguised as ordinary electronics – modified phones with enhanced security, tracking devices concealed as children's watches, surveillance detection tools that appeared to be everyday objects.

As they prepared to leave the office, Flynn placed a hand on Sam's shoulder. "The protocols are sound, but remember – the most effective security is what they don't expect."

"Meaning?"

"Meaning," Flynn said, glancing toward the door Danielle had just exited, "that a family aware of threats is already halfway to neutralizing them. Copenhagen changed things, Sam. The compartmentalization you've maintained isn't sustainable anymore."

The words echoed in Sam's mind later that night as he stood in the doorway of the guest room, watching his sleeping children. Ellie's analytical mind, already showing in her meticulous planning. Rae's linguistic facility, switching effortlessly between languages when they'd visited the international section of museums. Cade's remarkable memory and problem-solving abilities.

Danielle joined him, slipping her arm around his waist – the first voluntary contact she'd initiated since the revelation. "They're still just our children," she whispered. "Not assets or packages or capabilities."

"I know," Sam agreed. "That's why we protect them."

"Together," Danielle emphasized, though her tone made it clear this alliance was born of necessity rather than forgiveness. "No more separate worlds, Sam. Whatever this is, whatever happens next – we face it as a family."

Sam nodded, the weight of two worlds merging into one responsibility settling across his shoulders. "Together," he echoed, knowing that the East Coast trek had permanently altered their family's trajectory.

The children slept peacefully, unaware of the watchful eyes that had marked them – or of the protective measures now surrounding them.

In the morning, they would continue their journey, maintaining the appearance of an ordinary family vacation. They would visit Hershey's as promised, make chocolate bars, enjoy a memorable waffle breakfast at the Courtyard in Lancaster that would inspire them to buy their own waffle maker, take photographs, and create memories.

But underneath it all, a new vigilance had been established. The father who checked exits and assessed threats had become a father who understood those threats targeted his children specifically. The mother who organized activities and bandaged scraped knees had become a mother filled with righteous fury at those who would threaten her family.

The lesson of the East Coast trek was clear: the line between Sam's separate lives had not merely blurred – it had vanished entirely. And while their marriage faced its greatest challenge, their shared purpose had never been stronger.

Danielle's final words before sleep that night reflected this strange new reality: "I don't know if I can ever forgive you for the lies, Sam. But I will never let anyone take our children."

It was a beginning – not of reconciliation, but of a partnership forged in crisis. The road ahead would be difficult, their relationship forever altered, but their children would be protected.

By both of them.

Chapter 3
Paris At Midnight
July 2019

Moonlight spilled across the rooftops of Paris, casting long shadows that stretched like fingers across the ancient city. Sam Clayton stood on the balcony of their hotel room, watching the Eiffel Tower's hourly light show dance across the nighttime skyline. The champagne in his glass caught the reflection, creating tiny constellations that matched the distant stars.

Behind him, Danielle emerged from the bathroom wrapped in a hotel robe, her wet hair leaving dark patches on the white terry cloth. Twenty-five years of marriage had only deepened her beauty, the gentle lines around her eyes marking memories of laughter and concern in equal measure.

"Second thoughts about tomorrow?" she asked, joining him at the railing.

Sam smiled, the practiced expression that revealed nothing while appearing completely genuine. "Just thinking about how far we've come. From that little apartment in Plattsburgh to this." He gestured toward the Parisian panorama. "Sometimes I can hardly believe it."

This moment of peace—this celebration of their anniversary—should have been untainted. But beneath the veneer of the romantic getaway, a current of tension pulled at him. The timing of this trip hadn't been accidental. The invitation to the Montparnasse rooftop jazz reception tomorrow evening had arrived three weeks ago, precisely when Marcus mentioned a "French connection" requiring attention.

Inside their suite at the Hôtel du Rond Point des Champs Elysées, Sam's phone buzzed with a message. He ignored it, focusing instead on his wife's profile as she gazed out at the city.

"Remember when we could barely afford more than dinner at Arnie's on Margaret street for our anniversary?" Danielle smiled, the memory warming her eyes. "You wore that ridiculous tie your father gave you."

"It wasn't ridiculous, it was vintage," Sam protested with mock indignation. "Carmichael called it 'jazz formal.'"

Danielle laughed, a sound that still stirred something in him after all these years, despite the distance that had grown between them since that fateful trip in 2011. "Let's go for a walk," she suggested. "The night's too beautiful to waste."

Sam checked his watch—a handsome Tissot that had been his father's. It was nearly eleven. The message would have to wait. "Lead the way, Mrs. Clayton."

They strolled along the Seine, the water reflecting the city lights like black glass. Street musicians played for coins, the melody of an accordion drifting between ancient buildings. Couples sat entwined on benches, sharing wine and whispers.

"The kids called while you were in the shower," Sam said. "Cade's arguing with Carmichael about the proper way to record saxophone. Apparently, digital versus analog is causing quite the rift."

"Those two," Danielle smiled. "Like different versions of the same person. And Mackie?"

"Homesick. Nine is still young for a week away from mom and dad. But he perked up when Carleen mentioned the go-karts tomorrow."

They crossed Pont Neuf, pausing midway to look down the river. Notre-Dame stood in the distance, its Gothic silhouette a testament to survival and resilience. The scaffolding from April's fire created an eerie exoskeleton against the night sky.

"You know what Rae said?" Sam continued. "That there are thirty-seven distinct French accents, and she's determined to identify each one before we return."

Danielle laughed. "That girl and her languages. Did you know she's been teaching herself Italian? She says it helps her understand the roots of French better, but I think she's just showing off her language gene."

Sam nodded, thinking of his daughter's remarkable facility with languages. Seven languages by fifteen— an extraordinary gift that had developed naturally, without pressure. Just as Ellie's environmental insights had emerged, and Cade's intuitive grasp of patterns and systems.

They found themselves in a small plaza near Saint-Germain-des-Prés, where a jazz quartet played beneath strung lights. Sam guided Danielle into a slow dance, their bodies finding the familiar rhythm they'd perfected over years of kitchen swaying and basement dance parties with the kids.

"Remember our first dance?" Danielle asked, her cheek against his shoulder.

"How could I forget? Your cousin's wedding. You wore that blue dress."

"And you kept stepping on my toes."

"I've improved."

"Marginally."

As they danced, Sam scanned the plaza with practiced subtlety. Two men at a café table, too focused on their phones for the late hour. A woman sketching beneath a streetlamp who hadn't turned a page in fifteen minutes. Nothing conclusive, but enough to maintain awareness.

When they returned to the hotel, Sam checked his phone while Danielle readied for bed. The message was from Marcus: "Vermeer exhibition opens tomorrow. Don't miss the Girl with the Wineglass. Restoration reveals surprising details."

Sam deleted the message and joined his wife in bed, wrapping an arm around her waist as she drifted toward sleep. His mind raced through the implications. The Louvre's special exhibition of Dutch masters wasn't on their itinerary, but it would be now. The reference to restoration suggested new information had emerged, likely embedded in a forged painting.

Morning came with buttery sunlight and the distant sounds of Parisian traffic. They breakfasted on the hotel's rooftop, surrounded by climbing roses and the aroma of fresh coffee. Danielle wore a sundress that caught the light, her skin golden from summer days spent gardening at home.

"I've been thinking," Sam said, spreading marmalade on a croissant. "We should visit the Louvre today. They have a special exhibition of Dutch masters I'd love to see."

Danielle raised an eyebrow. "Art wasn't on the agenda. What happened to Montmartre and Sacré-Cœur?"

"We can do both. Start with the Louvre, then head to Montmartre for lunch?"

She studied him over her coffee cup, her gaze sharp with the practiced assessment she'd developed over eight years of partial knowledge. "Another one of Marcus's little projects?"

Sam paused, caught off guard by her directness. "What makes you say that?"

"Your phone buzzed last night. You only delete messages from Marcus." She sipped her coffee, eyes never leaving his. "So what is it this time? Information drop? Asset meeting?"

"Danielle—"

"Don't." Her voice remained calm, but carried a weight of accumulated frustration. "Not on our anniversary trip, Sam. Eight years of this is enough."

The tension that had simmered beneath their functional co-parenting arrangement rose to the surface. Sam set down his coffee cup carefully.

"It's important. I wouldn't have agreed otherwise."

Danielle considered this, then nodded once. "Fine. Louvre first, then Montmartre. But this time, I want to know exactly what we're walking into."

The Louvre hummed with tourists, a multilingual tapestry of movement and sound beneath I.M. Pei's glass pyramid. They joined the line, Sam's attention split between maintaining their cover as typical tourists and scanning for surveillance.

Inside, they wandered through galleries of Renaissance treasures, Sam guiding them gradually toward the special exhibition. Danielle paused before a Titian, captivated by the luminous quality of the skin tones.

"It's amazing how he captures light," she said. "Like it's coming from within the subject rather than falling on them."

Sam nodded, his gaze drifting to a man reading a museum guide too intensely, his posture too rigid for casual observation. "The Dutch masters took that technique even further," he said, gently steering her toward the exhibition entrance.

The special collection occupied a series of connected rooms, the lighting subdued to protect the centuries-old canvases. They moved slowly through the first gallery, admiring Rembrandt's dramatic use of shadow, the intimate domestic scenes of de Hooch.

In the third room, they found the Vermeers. "Girl with a Wineglass" hung on the far wall, its subject captured in a moment of hesitation, a young woman considering the glass offered by a gentleman visitor.

Sam positioned them before the painting, angling himself to both examine the work and monitor the room. The didactic panel noted recent restoration had revealed previously obscured details in the background.

"The craftsmanship is remarkable," Sam said, loud enough for nearby visitors to hear. "Look at how he renders the light through the glass."

Danielle stepped closer. "So what are we really looking for here?"

Sam pointed to the window depicted in the background. "See how he's painted the view outside? The buildings appear to be along a canal, but if you look carefully, the perspective is impossible. The waterline doesn't match the horizon."

As he spoke, Sam photographed the painting with his phone—a typical tourist behavior, though the camera's modified aperture would capture ultraviolet and infrared information invisible to the naked eye.

Danielle leaned in, her analytical mind engaging with the puzzle. "You're right. That's strange for Vermeer. He was usually obsessive about perspective."

"Exactly. And notice the pattern in the tablecloth—it's not consistent with his other works from this period."

A security guard drifted closer, his attention seemingly casual but his positioning strategic. Sam placed a hand on Danielle's back, gently guiding her toward the next painting.

"Let's see the others before the crowd gets too thick."

They completed their tour of the exhibition, Sam taking photographs of several other works to obscure his specific interest. As they left the Louvre, he felt the weight of observation—nothing overt, but the distinctive prickle at the back of his neck that had saved his life more than once.

"You've been watching our backs since we entered the museum," Danielle said quietly as they crossed the plaza. "How serious is this?"

Sam missed a step, recovering smoothly. "What makes you say that?"

"I've been watching you operate for eight years, Sam, even from the sidelines. You've checked reflective surfaces seven times. You positioned us with backs to walls in every room. You keep scanning exits." Her expression remained neutral, but her eyes held a challenge. "After all these years, I still don't know the whole truth, do I?"

For a moment, Sam considered his usual tactic of partial disclosure—the habit that had defined their relationship since 2011. But something in her steady gaze made him reconsider. "Not here," he said instead. "Let's get to Montmartre first."

They took a circuitous route, doubling back twice and changing Metro lines unnecessarily. By the time they emerged at the base of the hill crowned by Sacré-Cœur, Sam was reasonably confident they'd shed any surveillance.

They found a small café tucked away from the main tourist thoroughfare, selecting a table with a clear view of the street. After ordering, Sam leaned forward, lowering his voice.

"I'm sorry about bringing work into our anniversary."

Danielle sipped her water, her composure remarkable. "That's not what I'm upset about, and you know it. I'm tired of the fragments, Sam. The pieces of information you dole out when absolutely necessary. The constant 'need-to-know' basis after all these years."

"I've told you what I could—"

"You've told me what you felt was safe," she corrected. "There's a difference. For eight years, I've lived with security protocols, emergency contacts, safe houses, and contingency plans without ever understanding the full picture. Do you know what that's like?"

The waiter arrived with their lunch, forcing a pause in the conversation. When he departed, Danielle continued as if discussing the weather.

"Since the East Coast trip in 2011, I've been living with a ghost of a marriage. Co-parents who functionally share a life without sharing everything that matters."

Sam's mind raced. He had believed their compartmentalized life was working, despite the emotional distance. "I thought we had an understanding."

"We had a truce," Danielle broke off a piece of bread, considering it before responding. "One based on necessity, not choice. I stayed because of the kids, because I understand the importance of what you do, because I still love you despite everything. But I'm done with partial truths."

She met his eyes directly. "I want full access, Sam. No more filtering information through what you think I need to know."

The realization washed over him. She'd endured— not accepted—the arrangement for years. Had observed and cataloged and waited for him to truly trust her with the deeper truth.

"It could put you in danger," he said finally. "More than you already are."

"That's my decision to make, not yours." The conviction in her voice was unmistakable. "I made my choice eight years ago when I decided to stay after discovering your real work. I'm making another choice now."

Before he could answer, his phone vibrated with an incoming message. Marcus again: "Window closing. Confirmation needed by sunset."

Sam silenced the phone. "This isn't how I wanted this conversation to go."

"And yet here we are." She spread her hands in a gesture that encompassed the café, the trip, the years between them. "After all these years, I still don't know who I'm married to."

The question pierced him more deeply than he expected. Who indeed? The earth science teacher who loved his family and delighted in explaining geological wonders to students? Or the operative who had spent decades gathering intelligence on environmental data manipulation?

"Both versions are me," he said finally. "The teacher isn't a cover—it's who I wanted to be, who I became. But there's this other part too."

"Which I've only been allowed glimpses of since 2011." Not a question.

He nodded, watching her carefully.

"I want to know what we're really doing here, Sam. All of it. No more compartmentalization."

Sam weighed his options, aware they'd crossed a threshold that couldn't be reversed. "There's information embedded in the painting. The restoration note was code for new intelligence being available."

"And our anniversary trip?"

"Was genuine," he insisted. "But yes, the timing was...convenient."

Danielle absorbed this, her expression thoughtful rather than angry. After a long moment, she reached across the table and took his hand. "I want the full picture now. Not everything—I understand there are things you can't share. But enough that I'm not operating in the dark anymore."

Relief mingled with apprehension as Sam began to explain—carefully, selectively—about his work monitoring climate data manipulation by a group Marcus called the Consortium. How they falsified research to create artificial resource scarcities. How Sam's environmental expertise made him uniquely qualified to identify the tampering.

As he spoke, the weight of secrecy began to lift. Not completely—some compartments remained sealed—

but enough that he could breathe more freely than he had in years.

"So tonight's jazz reception?" Danielle asked when he finished.

"Operational. There's someone I need to meet."

She nodded, decision made. "Then I'll wear the blue dress. The one with the subtle pattern. It photographs poorly in low light—useful if anyone's watching."

Sam blinked, caught off-guard by her immediate shift toward operational thinking. "You don't have to be involved."

"I've been involved for twenty-five years," she said simply. "For the last eight, I've known enough to be worried but not enough to be truly helpful. That changes tonight."

They spent the afternoon exploring Montmartre as planned, but with a new understanding between them. Sam found himself sharing more than usual—pointing out surveillance cameras, explaining how certain cafés served as meeting points for various intelligence services.

Danielle absorbed it all with remarkable equanimity, occasionally asking questions that revealed she'd been piecing things together on her own for years.

As sunset approached, they returned to the hotel to prepare for the evening. Sam secured his modified camera and phone while Danielle dressed. When she emerged in the blue dress—elegant, sophisticated, and indeed difficult to photograph clearly—he felt a surge of pride and concern.

"You understand this changes things," he said as they prepared to leave. "There's no going back to the way it's been."

"I've been waiting for this conversation for years, Sam." She adjusted his tie—a subtle blue that complemented her dress. "For full disclosure, not just crumbs of information when absolutely necessary."

The Montparnasse rooftop jazz reception glittered with Paris's cultural elite. Musicians, artists, curators, and wealthy patrons mingled amid champagne and sunset views. Sam guided Danielle through the crowd with practiced ease, introducing her to acquaintances who believed him to be a visiting American academic.

They separated casually, Danielle engaging a musicologist in conversation about jazz influences on French cinema while Sam drifted toward the bar. As he ordered, a slender man in a well-cut suit appeared beside him.

"The Vermeer was illuminating," the man said in accented English. "Though some question its provenance."

"Authenticity often lies beneath the surface," Sam replied, completing the exchange protocol.

"Jules Renard." The man extended his hand. "I admired your paper on coastal erosion patterns last year."

"Sam Clayton. And my wife, Danielle." He gestured toward her across the room. "She's the real scientist in the family."

They moved to a quieter corner as the band began their set, the sultry notes of a saxophone weaving through the evening air.

"The painting contains shipping manifests," Renard said without preamble. "Movements of specialized equipment to monitoring stations around the Arctic Circle. The data being collected isn't what's being reported."

"Temperature variations?"

"And oceanic salinity levels. The discrepancies are subtle but consistent. Creating a pattern of apparent freshwater intrusion that doesn't align with actual ice melt rates."

Sam absorbed this, connecting it to anomalies he'd noted in published research. "Who's behind the falsification?"

"The installation carries Kessler Global Consulting markers. But there are layers beneath that."

Kessler. The name triggered connections to other operations, other data points. Richard Kessler, former CIA director, now running a private global consulting firm with unprecedented access to governments and corporations worldwide.

"The documentation?"

"Secured location. I can provide access tonight, after this reception concludes."

Sam nodded, mentally adjusting the evening's timeline. "My wife will need to accompany us. She's fully operational."

Renard hesitated. "Is that wise?"

"She's been aware and partially involved since 2011. Tonight she's fully in."

The Frenchman studied him for a moment, then nodded. "The Night Owl café in Saint-Germain. Midnight."

As Renard melted back into the crowd, Danielle appeared at Sam's side, timing her approach perfectly. "Well?"

"We have a meeting at midnight. You're coming with me."

She took a champagne flute from a passing waiter. "Of course I am."

They remained at the reception for another hour, maintaining their cover while Sam covertly photographed several attendees connected to environmental policy organizations. As they prepared to leave, the band struck up "La Vie en Rose." Sam extended his hand.

"One dance before we go?"

Danielle stepped into his arms with practiced ease. As they moved across the floor, she leaned close to his ear. "The woman in the green dress by the railing —she's been watching you all evening."

Sam turned them gently to get a better view. "Good catch. Cultural attaché to the Russian embassy, according to her credentials. But that's not her real position."

"How can you tell?"

"The shoes. Too practical for someone whose job is attending parties. And she has calluses on her right hand consistent with regular firearm training."

Danielle raised an eyebrow. "You noticed her calluses from across the room?"

"I noticed them when she handed me my coat check ticket earlier."

The song ended, and they made their exit, taking a deliberately complex route to the Night Owl café. The small jazz venue was tucked between a bookshop and a tobacconist, its blue neon sign flickering against the night.

Renard was waiting in a booth at the back, a manila envelope beside his coffee cup. He nodded to Danielle. "Madame Clayton. Jules Renard."

"A pleasure," she replied in flawless French. "Though I suspect that's not your real name."

A flicker of surprise crossed Renard's face before he composed himself. "Perceptive. Jules Renard was a French writer known for his keen observations of human nature."

"And his meticulous journals," Danielle added. "Which revealed far more in subtext than in direct statement."

Renard smiled appreciatively. "Your wife is remarkable," he said to Sam.

"You have no idea," Sam replied.

The Frenchman slid the envelope across the table. "This contains access credentials for a research facility outside Paris. The security protocols change at two AM for system maintenance. There's a twenty-minute window when the secondary systems are vulnerable."

Sam checked his watch. Just over an hour to prepare. "Location?"

"Meudon. Former observatory now converted to climate research center. The target is in the secure server room, level B2."

"Surveillance?"

"Standard motion and heat detection. Nothing you can't handle with this." Renard produced a small device resembling a key fob. "Temporary electromagnetic disruption. Three-minute window per use, five-minute recharge."

Sam pocketed the device. "Extraction protocol?"

"The same café where we met this afternoon. I'll be there from six to seven tomorrow morning."

As Renard stood to leave, he hesitated. "One more thing. The Girl with a Wineglass isn't what it appears to be. The painting itself is a forgery—a masterful one, but still a forgery."

"How do you know?" Danielle asked.

"Because I painted it." With a slight nod, he disappeared into the Paris night.

Sam turned to Danielle, whose expression balanced surprise with analytical assessment. "A forger working with intelligence services. That's...unexpected."

"Art and espionage have a long history together," Sam said, examining the contents of the envelope. "Especially art forgery. The skills transfer remarkably well."

"So we're breaking into a research facility in the middle of the night," Danielle said matter-of-factly. "Not exactly what I imagined for our anniversary."

Sam glanced up, concern crossing his features. "We can find another way. You don't have to—"

"Sam." She placed her hand over his. "Twenty-five years. Eight of them spent in this strange half-life. If we're going to do this, let's do it together. Properly."

The research facility in Meudon rose against the night sky like a fortress of glass and steel, its architecture a stark contrast to the surrounding historic buildings. Sam parked their rental car on a side street two blocks away, out of range of security cameras.

"Your bag," he said, handing Danielle a small backpack. "Flashlight, communications unit, gloves. Stay close and follow my lead."

She accepted the equipment with remarkable calm. "Just like chaperoning the science club field trip to the Adirondack Science Center."

"Slightly higher stakes," he said with a half-smile.

"Debatable. Have you seen what happens when thirty teenagers get unlimited access to liquid nitrogen?"

They approached the facility from the southwest corner, using the shadow of an adjacent building for cover. The perimeter fence posed little challenge—a maintenance gate with a keypad lock that yielded to the access code from Renard's envelope.

The real security began at the building itself. Motion sensors swept the grounds at regular intervals, forcing them to time their movements precisely.

"Now," Sam whispered, and they sprinted across the open space to a service entrance. Another code, another door unlocked. Inside, the facility hummed with the sound of environmental systems and distant machinery.

"Cameras?" Danielle whispered.

Sam pointed to a small device on his belt. "Scrambler. Creates a loop in the feed. As long as we're within thirty feet, they see empty hallways."

They moved through the building like shadows, descending staircases rather than using elevators. Sam navigated with the confidence of someone working from precise intelligence, checking his watch periodically to track their timing against the security protocol changes.

At level B2, they encountered the first significant obstacle—a biometric scanner guarding the server room door.

"The envelope didn't include fingerprints," Danielle observed dryly.

Sam removed a thin film from an inside pocket of his jacket. "Synthetic fingerprint overlay. Renard included the profile of someone with access—Dr. Emmanuel Laurent."

"When were you going to tell me about this part of teaching earth science?"

"It never seemed to fit in the faculty meeting agenda."

The scanner accepted the synthetic print, and the door unlocked with a pneumatic hiss. Inside, rows of servers hummed beneath blue emergency lighting.

"Target server?" Danielle asked, immediately focused on the task.

"Section C, rack 4. Should be labeled 'AGCM-Arctic.'"

They located the server quickly, Sam connecting a specialized drive to its diagnostic port. The device bypassed standard security protocols, creating a temporary shadow access point.

"Download initiating," Sam murmured. "Four minutes to completion."

Danielle positioned herself near the door, monitoring the hallway through a narrow window. "Movement at the end of the corridor. Security patrol ahead of schedule."

Sam checked the download progress. "Two minutes remaining. We need a distraction."

Without hesitation, Danielle removed a small aerosol can from her bag. "Smoke detector?"

"Northeast corner."

She moved quickly to the detector, spraying a precise amount of aerosol beneath it. Within seconds, the alarm triggered, lights flashing as a computerized voice announced a fire alert in French.

The patrol diverted toward the fire control panel, giving Sam the time needed to complete the download and disconnect the drive.

"Innovative," he commented as they slipped from the server room.

"Chemistry teacher," she replied simply.

They followed the evacuation route along with confused night staff responding to the alarm, blending perfectly into the small crowd that gathered in the parking lot. In the confusion, they slipped away, walking unhurriedly toward their car.

Only when they were miles away, heading back toward Paris, did Danielle break the silence.

"That was actually rather exhilarating."

Sam glanced at her, noting the flush in her cheeks, the brightness in her eyes. "It can be. That's part of the danger."

"The intellectual challenge, the physical demands, the importance of the work—I understand why you do it." She looked out at the passing countryside. "What I don't understand is why you've kept me at arm's length all these years."

Sam tightened his grip on the steering wheel. "After what happened in 2011, I thought limited knowledge was the best compromise. You knew enough to be safe, but not enough to be fully implicated."

"Don't pretend this was about protection," she said, her voice gentle but firm. "This is about trust. About whether you see me as a true partner."

He was silent for a long moment. "I was afraid," he admitted finally. "Afraid that bringing you fully in would erase the last boundary between my worlds. That there would be no safe, normal life to return to."

"And now?"

"Now I'm terrified that I've crossed a line that can't be uncrossed. That I've finally brought you completely into something dangerous that should have remained partially separate from our family."

Danielle reached over, covering his hand with hers. "You didn't bring me into this, Sam. I was already here. The only difference is now I can help as a full partner instead of a reluctant ally."

They reached Paris as dawn broke over the city, the early light painting the ancient buildings in gold. After securing the data drive in a specially designed compartment in Sam's luggage, they walked to the café where Renard waited.

The handoff was quick and professional—the drive exchanged for an envelope containing first-class tickets to London, their extraction route home.

"Your wife is a natural," Renard commented quietly as Danielle ordered coffee at the counter.

"She shouldn't have to be," Sam replied.

"And yet she is. Perhaps the distance you've maintained isn't as necessary as you thought."

When Danielle returned with their coffee, Renard bid them farewell. "Until our paths cross again."

"I'd ask if that's likely," Danielle said, "but I suspect I know the answer."

Left alone, they sat in comfortable silence, watching Paris awaken around them. The weight of the night's revelations—both operational and personal—settled between them, changing the contours of their relationship in ways Sam was only beginning to understand.

"What happens now?" Danielle asked eventually.

Sam thought of the data they'd extracted, the forged painting, the complex web of manipulation extending from Paris to the Arctic. But mostly he thought of the woman beside him, who had walked into his secret world with remarkable courage and adaptability.

"We finish our anniversary trip," he said, reaching for her hand. "We see the Musée d'Orsay this afternoon as planned. We have dinner at that restaurant on the Seine. And we talk—really talk—about what this means for us."

"And then?"

"Then we go home to our children. And I stop compartmentalizing. No more separate worlds."

Danielle squeezed his hand, her smile both understanding and warning. "I've been waiting for this conversation for years, Sam Clayton. Don't think for a moment we're done with it."

Above them, the Paris morning bloomed into brilliant blue, a new day dawning on a marriage transformed by truth fully shared at last.

Chapter 4
The Caribbean Cipher
July 2021

Sultry Caribbean air clung to Sam's skin as he surveyed the eerily still waters of Carlisle Bay. Flawless turquoise waves reflected the blinding morning sun, creating a paradise that concealed darker purposes. Standing on the beach outside their resort, he watched Cade and Mackie race toward the water with unbridled enthusiasm while Ellie set up her research equipment on a weathered wooden table beneath a cluster of palms.

Caribbean vacations had never been their family tradition, making this Barbados trip an effective operational cover. For a decade, Sam had maintained a fragile balance—giving Danielle enough information to protect their family while keeping operational details compartmentalized. After her demand for greater inclusion in Paris two years ago, this trip represented a significant shift—

bringing her into active field operations rather than just providing background awareness.

He spotted Danielle approaching, her chestnut curls catching the tropical breeze. After ten years of strained cooperation since that devastating East Coast trek discovery, her presence in the field still triggered conflicting emotions—professional concern and personal relief that their fractured relationship had evolved into something functional, if not fully healed.

"Morning observations?" she asked, her perceptive brown eyes scanning the bay alongside him, demonstrating the analytical precision that had made her a valuable, if reluctant, operational partner for years.

"Something's off with the water temperature readings." Sam gestured toward Ellie's monitoring equipment. "The official reports say 82 degrees, but Ellie's showing nearly 85 consistently since yesterday."

"Three degrees doesn't seem significant for Caribbean waters in July," Danielle noted as she sipped her coffee, the scientific mind that had proven useful during their limited collaborative work over the years immediately engaging with the problem.

"It is when it's localized to specific coordinates and all official monitoring buoys are reporting unusually consistent readings. Nature isn't that precise." Sam lowered his voice as Rae approached, wearing a University of Plattsburgh t-shirt over her swimsuit.

"Dad, did you see the tourist brochure about Harrison's Cave?" Rae asked, her eyes holding a subtle intensity that signaled more than casual interest. "There's a special guided tour this afternoon that explores 'the hidden water systems of Barbados.'"

Sam nodded, catching her meaning immediately. Rae had overheard his conversation with Dr. Coraline Waters yesterday—officially a marine biologist, unofficially his local contact. "I'll book it when the front desk opens."

Danielle watched this exchange with quiet understanding, the years since 2011 having taught her to recognize operational communications embedded in casual conversation. After their world-shattering confrontation a decade ago, followed by years of limited participation while co-parenting their children with emotional distance, this vacation marked her first significant field operation—a milestone in their complex journey.

"Ellie's work with that new monitoring equipment isn't just a college project, is it?" Danielle asked after Rae had walked toward her siblings, her tone reflecting years of learning to balance maternal concern with operational necessity.

Sam met her eyes, remembering Paris two years ago when she'd finally demanded full access after years of living with partial information. "No. It's not."

Sunlight fractured through the crystal waters as Sam descended toward the reef, adjusting his mask while monitoring the dive computer strapped to his wrist. Twenty feet below, Ellie glided with remarkable confidence for a 19-year-old, her research-grade underwater camera capturing images of the coral formations. To casual observers, they were environmentally conscious tourists documenting reef health. To Sam, this was Ellie's first operational dive.

The wreck of the Berwyn loomed ahead, a freighter deliberately sunk in 1919 to create an artificial reef. Now home to vibrant marine life, it also served as the anchor point for something far more recent. Sam signaled Ellie to follow as he navigated around the rusted hull to the shadowed northern side.

There, partially concealed by coral growth, sat the first anomaly—a cylindrical object mounted to the ship's hull. Too modern for the century-old wreck, too sophisticated for typical marine research equipment. Ellie immediately began photographing while Sam examined the device, careful not to touch it. The casing appeared commercial-grade, indistinguishable from university research equipment, but the precision mounting and camouflaged power supply told a different story.

Sam detected movement in his peripheral vision and turned to see Danielle approaching. Despite years of mainly desk-based involvement with his work, she moved with natural grace through the water. He'd initially opposed her joining this particular dive, but her chemistry background—which had proven valuable in their limited collaborative work over the past decade—was essential for identifying potential data falsification in water analysis samples. This inclusion marked another step in bridging the gap that had existed between them since that fateful 2011 discovery.

Danielle pointed to something beyond the device—a thin cable running along the ocean floor, partially buried in sand. Sam nodded and they followed its path, discovering it connected to a network of similar monitoring devices positioned strategically around the wreck site. Each had been carefully placed to appear part of legitimate research efforts, yet their arrangement created a sophisticated surveillance grid covering the bay.

After documenting each device, they ascended slowly, following proper decompression protocols. The family surfaced some distance from the beach where Cade awaited with the small rental boat. At fourteen, Mackie remained on shore with Rae, unaware of the dive's true purpose.

"Found something interesting?" Cade asked casually as they climbed aboard, his voice carrying the forced nonchalance of someone practicing operational security—skills he'd absorbed through the years growing up in a household governed by subtle security protocols.

"Fascinating coral formations," Sam replied, maintaining their cover story while helping Ellie with her equipment.

Once safely underway, Ellie pulled the camera's memory card and handed it to Cade. At seventeen, his programming skills had developed remarkably, particularly in data analysis algorithms that would have impressed professional cryptographers.

"The device configurations match the patterns we found in the monitoring reports," Ellie said, her voice lowered despite being in open water. "They're collecting legitimate data, but transmitting manipulated readings."

"The question is why," Danielle added, removing her dive cap and shaking out her wet hair. After a decade of limited engagement with Sam's operational world, her analytical skills remained sharp, focused now on a real-world problem rather than the theoretical briefings she'd received over the years.

Sam watched as Cade connected the memory card to a tablet disguised as standard vacation equipment. "It's not just here. I've been comparing the anomalies with global patterns. There are similar inconsistencies in monitoring stations throughout the Caribbean, Gulf of Mexico, and Mediterranean."

"All prime tourist destinations," Ellie noted.

"And all regions with significant shipping lanes, fishing industries, and desalination dependencies," Sam added. "The same pattern we found in the Arctic data."

The mention of the Arctic triggered a shared understanding among them. The Paris operation two years ago had yielded evidence of similar manipulations in northern waters—the same operation where Danielle had confronted Sam about years of partial information, demanding full access after eight years of being kept at arm's length from operational details.

"How are they transmitting the data?" Danielle asked, her scientific mind focusing on practical mechanisms—the kind of pragmatic approach that had made her contributions valuable during her limited involvement over the years.

Cade tapped through several screens on his tablet. "That's what's interesting. The devices are dual-channel. They're collecting accurate readings locally while transmitting altered data to official monitoring networks. But they're storing the real data too."

"For what purpose?" Ellie wondered.

"Insurance," Sam replied. "Whoever's behind this wants both the manipulated numbers for public consumption and the real data for their own use. It gives them an information advantage."

As they approached the shore, Sam noticed two men in technical diving gear preparing to enter the water from a sleek boat anchored on the bay's eastern edge. Their equipment appeared recreational, but the precision of their preparation and the specialized configuration of their gear signaled professional training. Their timing—arriving just as Sam's family departed the wreck site—suggested surveillance rather than coincidence.

"Time to head back," Sam announced casually. "We've got that cave tour this afternoon."

Harrison's Cave sprawled beneath the island's surface like a forgotten cathedral, its limestone chambers illuminated by strategic lighting that transformed mineral deposits into otherworldly sculptures. The family joined a small tour group led by a guide whose enthusiasm for the cave system seemed genuine.

"These formations took thousands of years to create," the guide explained, gesturing to stalactites hanging from the ceiling. "And the underground streams you see here form part of Barbados' complex freshwater system."

Sam studied the underground waterway as they moved deeper into the cave system. What appeared to tourists as a natural wonder served additional purposes. The cave's natural limestone filtered rainwater into the island's aquifer, providing much of the local drinking water. Any manipulation of climate data would directly impact water management policies for the entire region.

When the tour reached a spectacular domed chamber called the "Great Hall," the guide allowed visitors to explore independently for a few minutes. Sam seized the opportunity to separate from the group, moving toward a maintenance door partially concealed behind a rock formation. Rae fell into step beside him, creating a natural conversational barrier.

"Mom's keeping Mackie occupied with the crystal formations," she reported quietly. "Ellie and Cade are watching the guide."

Sam nodded, appreciating how naturally his family had adapted to operational awareness over the years. Since Danielle's traumatic discovery in 2011, security protocols had become part of their children's upbringing, even if the full context remained undefined until more recently. Reaching the maintenance door, he extracted a small tool from his pocket that resembled a tourist's penlight. The lock yielded quickly to his expertise, allowing them to slip through unnoticed.

The maintenance tunnel beyond was utilitarian and dimly lit, housing electrical systems and water monitoring equipment. Sam moved directly to a control panel mounted on the wall, its modern digital display contrasting with the raw stone surroundings.

"The island's main aquifer monitoring station," Sam explained as he connected a specialized drive disguised as a common USB stick to the system's maintenance port. "This tracks all groundwater data for central Barbados."

"Why would anyone manipulate cave water measurements?" Rae asked, her voice barely above a whisper.

"It's not about the measurements themselves, but how they're interpreted," Sam replied, watching data stream across his device. "Climate models use the relationship between air temperature, precipitation, and groundwater to make predictions about drought cycles and water availability. Change one variable, and you change policy decisions worth billions."

The drive completed its download just as footsteps echoed from further down the tunnel. Sam disconnected quickly, pocketing the device as Rae positioned herself naturally between him and the approaching figures.

Two maintenance workers rounded the corner, their uniforms bearing the logo of Barbados Water Authority. The older man frowned at finding tourists in a restricted area.

"You shouldn't be here," he stated firmly, his Bajan accent thick with authority.

"My apologies," Sam responded with embarrassed tourist charm. "My daughter's doing a research project on limestone caverns, and we got turned around looking for the restrooms."

The younger worker seemed satisfied with this explanation, but the older man's eyes narrowed slightly, examining Sam with subtle scrutiny. After a tense moment, he gestured toward the door. "Tour's that way."

As they rejoined the tour group, Rae whispered, "He didn't believe you."

"No," Sam agreed. "He didn't."

The beachfront restaurant at Sam Lord's Castle resort offered perfect surveillance coverage of the bay while providing excellent seafood. The family occupied a corner table on the open-air deck, their dinner conversation carefully balanced between normal vacation topics and coded updates—a communication style they'd perfected through years of living with security awareness.

"The marine photography turned out beautifully," Ellie commented, scrolling through selected images on her camera that she'd shown the waiter earlier. "Especially those unusual formations near the shipwreck."

Sam understood she was referring to the underwater monitoring devices. "I'm curious about the technical specifications. Cade, did you have a chance to look at them more closely?"

Cade nodded, his expression casual though his eyes held focused intensity. "The configuration is interesting. They're running a modified version of standard oceanographic software, but with custom modifications to the reporting algorithms."

"Environmental engineering at its finest," Danielle commented, maintaining their cover conversation while signaling her understanding. After a decade of forced cooperation with Sam's work, she had developed a natural fluency in these coded exchanges, finding unexpected satisfaction in finally applying her knowledge to field operations.

Mackie, now fifteen and increasingly observant, glanced between his family members with subtle curiosity. Though not explicitly included in operational discussions, his natural aptitude for spatial relationships had already manifested in detailed sketches of the resort's layout, complete with security camera positions he'd unconsciously included through pure observation.

"Think we could get a map of those dive sites?" Mackie asked innocently. "I'd like to create a 3D model when we get home."

Before Sam could answer, he noticed Dr. Coraline Waters entering the restaurant. The marine biologist's presence was expected—they had arranged to meet—but the two men following her at a discreet distance triggered Sam's internal alarms. The same technical divers from the bay earlier, now dressed in casual resort wear that didn't quite conceal their professional posture.

"Rae, why don't you and Mackie check out the dessert options?" Sam suggested, keeping his tone light while catching Danielle's eye.

As the younger children moved toward the display case, Coraline approached their table with professional casualness, her sundress and wide-brimmed hat making her look like any other tourist.

"The Clayton family, right?" she said warmly, extending her hand. "I believe we met at the marine conservation presentation yesterday. I'm Coraline Waters."

"Of course," Danielle replied smoothly. "Please join us. We were just discussing the reef preservation efforts."

As Coraline took the empty seat, she positioned herself with her back to the entrance, allowing Sam to maintain visual contact with the men who had followed her. They had taken a table near the bar, ostensibly casual while maintaining clear sightlines to Coraline.

"Your daughter's monitoring project is quite impressive," Coraline said, nodding toward Ellie. "Not many undergraduates show such technical proficiency."

"She's always been environmentally conscious," Sam replied, the proud father comment serving as both truth and cover.

"I noticed you were diving near the Berwyn wreck this morning," Coraline continued, her voice conversational while her eyes conveyed greater significance. "Find anything interesting?"

"Unusual current patterns," Sam replied carefully. "And some unexpected equipment installations."

Coraline nodded slightly. "My research team has been tracking anomalies in the data stream for months. The official reports show stable temperatures with normal fluctuations, but our independent measurements indicate organized manipulation."

"Who would benefit from falsifying ocean temperature data?" Danielle asked, her chemistry background and years of peripheral involvement with Sam's work making this a genuine question despite her awareness of the larger conspiracy.

"Follow the resource allocation," Coraline answered quietly. "Caribbean nations base their water management, fishing regulations, and tourism development on climate predictions. Manipulate those predictions, and you control economic development across the region."

Sam noticed one of the men at the bar speaking into his watch—too deliberately for checking the time. "Your colleagues seem interested in our conversation."

Coraline didn't turn. "Not colleagues. I've had a shadow since publishing my recent paper questioning the consistency of regional water temperature reporting."

"The same paper that lost your university funding," Ellie added, demonstrating her research thoroughness.

"The official reason was budget cuts," Coraline confirmed with a tight smile. "The unofficial reason was pressure from several corporate donors with interests in regional water rights."

Rae and Mackie returned to the table, Mackie carrying a dessert menu while Rae subtly signaled additional surveillance—a slight tilt of her head indicating new observers at the entrance. Sam registered the information without obvious reaction, maintaining their casual dinner persona.

"Dr. Waters was just explaining how ocean temperature affects the entire island ecosystem," Sam said for Mackie's benefit.

"Including the cave systems we visited today?" Mackie asked, his question innocently perceptive.

"Especially those," Coraline confirmed. "Barbados sits on a massive limestone formation that filters rainwater through the very caves you toured. The entire freshwater system depends on predictable rainfall patterns, which in turn depend on accurate climate modeling."

As their conversation continued, Sam noticed the men at the bar had been joined by a third individual —a woman in business casual attire who didn't fit the tourist demographic. Her brief conversation with the men followed by their immediate departure triggered Sam's operational instincts.

"I believe we should continue this discussion somewhere less crowded," Sam suggested, meeting Coraline's eyes with subtle urgency.

Coraline understood immediately. "There's a wonderful viewpoint just down the beach. Perfect for watching the sunset."

The family gathered their belongings casually, Sam leaving cash to cover their bill rather than waiting for the check. As they exited the restaurant, Rae fell into step beside Mackie, her protective positioning subtle but deliberate. Ellie and Cade flanked Coraline while Sam and Danielle led the group, their formation providing maximum security while appearing entirely natural—a pattern developed through years of living with security awareness even without explicit training.

The "viewpoint" turned out to be a small gazebo set slightly apart from the main beach, offering both privacy and clear sightlines in all directions. Once certain they hadn't been followed, Coraline produced a small tablet from her bag.

"These are the actual readings from monitoring stations across the Caribbean for the past eighteen months," she explained, displaying a series of data charts. "And these are the officially published reports for the same period."

The discrepancies were immediately apparent— subtle enough to appear as normal variation to casual observation, but forming a clear pattern when viewed comprehensively.

"They're manipulating seasonal predictions," Cade observed, studying the algorithms with impressive speed. "Creating the appearance of coming water shortages in specific regions."

"Regions with valuable development rights and desalination contracts pending," Coraline confirmed. "Whoever controls the predictive models essentially dictates resource allocation policies worth billions."

"The same pattern we found in the Arctic and Mediterranean data," Sam noted, connecting this operation to their previous discoveries.

"And likely the same actors," Danielle added, her analytical mind assembling the global picture. After a decade of limited operational involvement— primarily analyzing data safely from home rather than in the field—the satisfaction of direct participation brought unexpected pleasure.

"The question is how they're maintaining the technical implementation across such diverse regions," Ellie said, examining the monitoring device specifications. "These installations require sophisticated equipment and trained personnel."

"That's where this comes in," Coraline said, revealing a small data drive. "I've identified a series of shell companies supplying 'research equipment' to academic institutions and government agencies across the region. They all trace back to a single corporate entity—Kessler Global Consulting."

The name registered immediately with Sam and Danielle, connecting directly to their Paris operation two years ago, where Danielle had finally demanded full access after years of limited information. Before they could discuss further, Sam's phone vibrated with an incoming message—a simple numerical sequence that translated to an emergency evacuation code from Flynn.

"We need to move," Sam announced, shifting immediately to operational mode. "Coraline, you're coming with us."

"What's happening?" Mackie asked, his adolescent curiosity tinged with growing awareness.

"Change of plans," Sam replied calmly, already guiding the group toward the beach access path rather than returning to the main resort. "We're taking an evening boat tour."

Danielle understood immediately, taking Mackie's hand while maintaining a relaxed façade. Her decade of living with security protocols—even at the periphery of Sam's work—had prepared her for moments like this. "I hear the bioluminescent bay is spectacular at night."

As they moved swiftly but casually along the shoreline, Sam explained to Coraline in low tones. "Your research has triggered more than academic interest. My contact indicates a technical team has been dispatched to secure the monitoring network—and eliminate security concerns."

"Like me," Coraline concluded grimly.

"And potentially us, now that we've been seen with you," Sam confirmed, leading them toward a small marina beyond the resort property.

When they reached the docks, Cade moved with surprising confidence toward a specific slip containing a modest but well-maintained motorboat.

The teenager produced a key from his pocket and began preparing the vessel with practiced efficiency.

"Sailing lessons paying off," Sam commented with paternal pride that wasn't entirely for show.

Within minutes, Cade had the boat ready while the others boarded casually, maintaining the appearance of a standard evening excursion. As they pulled away from the dock, Sam noted a group of men moving purposefully along the beach toward their previous location.

"Just in time," he observed quietly to Danielle.

"You knew this might happen," she responded. Not a question, but a realization.

"I suspected the possibility," Sam acknowledged. "The children's inclusion was both necessity and preparation." Seeing her expression, he added, "They've been involved since Copenhagen, Danielle. We've both known that since 2011, whether we fully acknowledged it or not."

As the boat moved farther from shore, Ellie and Cade collaborated on the navigation while Rae kept Mackie engaged in conversation at the bow, allowing the adults privacy for operational discussion.

"The marina rental is under an alias," Sam explained to Coraline. "We'll make for Oistins on the south coast where I have arrangements for your extraction to Miami."

"My research—" Coraline began.

"Is on the drive you gave us," Sam finished. "And will reach the proper authorities. Your priority now is safety."

Danielle watched her children working together—Ellie's environmental knowledge guiding Cade's technical expertise as they plotted the most efficient course, Rae's linguistic skills evident as she explained marine terminology to Mackie in both English and Spanish to reinforce his language studies. Each applying their natural talents to the situation with remarkable adaptability, skills they'd been cultivating throughout their upbringing in a household defined by security awareness since 2011.

"They're good at this," she observed softly. "Too good for it to be coincidence."

Sam met her eyes, understanding the deeper question. "Their abilities were always there. This just gives them purpose."

"And puts them in danger," Danielle countered, though without the accusation that would have accompanied such words a decade ago. Years of maintaining a careful partnership for their children's sake had tempered her anger, if not fully healed the breach.

"The danger exists regardless," Sam replied. "The difference is now they're prepared."

As the coastline receded behind them, the brilliant Caribbean sunset painted the western sky in fiery orange and deep purple. The momentary beauty provided stark contrast to the operation unfolding around them—a family vacation transformed into an extraction mission through waters concealing falsified data that affected millions.

Coraline joined them at the stern, her expression resolute despite the abrupt upheaval of her life. "Your children—they've done this before?"

"Not exactly," Sam answered. "But they've been preparing without knowing it."

"And now?" Coraline asked.

"Now they know more," Danielle replied, watching as Mackie pointed out a navigation buoy to Rae— one of the very monitoring points they'd been investigating. Her gaze reflected a decade of complicated emotions, of raising children with security awareness while maintaining emotional distance from her husband. "They've grown up with protocols and awareness, but this is different."

Sam followed her gaze to their children—Ellie checking water samples, Cade monitoring their digital signature, Rae and Mackie maintaining lookout while disguising it as tourism enthusiasm. Their inherited talents now directed toward a purpose none of them had chosen, yet all seemed naturally suited for.

"We protect them by preparing them," Sam said quietly. "It's all we can do."

As their boat cut through the darkening waters toward Oistins, Danielle placed her hand over Sam's on the gunwale—the first genuine gesture of connection they'd shared in years. "Then we prepare them together. No more separate worlds."

Behind them, the lights of Sam Lord's Castle twinkled along the shoreline like stars fallen to earth, the idyllic resort now a marker of their family's transformation. What had begun as a traumatic discovery in 2011, followed by years of functional co-parenting with emotional distance, was now evolving into something more integrated—not by Sam's design, but by necessity and their children's remarkable capabilities.

The Caribbean operation had crystallized something Sam had suspected since their world fractured in 2011: his children's talents weren't random genetic fortune but inherited aptitudes carefully nurtured through years of subtle preparation. Whether by design or destiny, the Clayton family had become more than individual operatives—they were becoming a unit with complementary skills and shared purpose.

As night enveloped the boat, stars emerging in the tropical sky, Sam contemplated the implications of this evolution. The line between protection and preparation had blurred, between childhood and operational awareness. There was no returning to the compartmentalized lives he'd maintained before Danielle's discovery a decade ago.

The Caribbean cipher had been broken, revealing not just manipulated climate data, but the undeniable truth about his family's future.

As they approached the southern coast, lights from fishing boats twinkling on the horizon, Cade motioned Sam toward the navigation console. The teenager had connected his tablet to the boat's systems, displaying a detailed mapping of transmissions from the coastal monitoring network.

"I've been tracking the data patterns," Cade explained, his voice holding the focused intensity that emerged when solving complex problems. "The manipulations aren't random—they're creating artificial patterns that influence predictive models."

Sam studied the display, impressed with Cade's analysis. "Predictive models that determine resource allocation decisions."

"Exactly," Cade confirmed. "But there's something else. The monitoring stations aren't just transmitting false data—they're collecting comprehensive environmental readings, far beyond what's necessary for temperature monitoring."

"What kind of readings?" Danielle asked, joining them at the console, her scientific expertise—kept sharp through years of limited operational involvement—immediately engaging with the problem.

"Everything," Cade replied. "Water composition, mineral content, biological activity, acoustic mapping. They're creating a complete environmental surveillance network disguised as climate research."

The implications were significant—whoever controlled this network possessed detailed intelligence on everything from shipping movements to underwater resource deposits, all while manipulating public climate data to influence policy decisions.

"The perfect information advantage," Sam concluded. "They see the real data while everyone else acts on the manipulated predictions."

As they discussed the implications, lights appeared behind them—a fast-moving vessel approaching from the direction they'd come. Its running lights were minimal, its approach deliberate and rapid.

"We've got company," Ellie announced from her observation position.

Sam quickly assessed their options. "Cade, maximum sustainable speed. Rae, get Mackie and Dr. Waters below deck. Ellie, prepare the diversion package."

The family responded with remarkable coordination, each understanding their role without detailed explanation. As Cade accelerated the boat, Ellie retrieved a waterproof case from their equipment store, extracting devices that resembled standard emergency flares.

"Modified signal markers," Sam explained to Danielle. "They'll create multiple heat signatures on any tracking systems."

The pursuing vessel continued to gain ground, its superior engines providing significant advantage. As it drew within three hundred yards, a spotlight snapped on, illuminating their boat in harsh white light.

"Now, Ellie," Sam directed.

Ellie deployed three devices overboard in different directions, each activating upon water contact to create thermal and electronic signatures mimicking small vessels. Simultaneously, Cade executed a sharp turn toward a cluster of fishing boats near the coastline.

"We'll use the local traffic for cover," Sam explained as their boat sliced through the dark water.

"Standard watercraft are difficult to distinguish at night."

The pursuing vessel hesitated momentarily as its tracking systems registered multiple targets, then divided its focus between them. Sam used the momentary confusion to guide their boat into the pattern of local fishing vessels returning to harbor.

"They're still following," Danielle observed as the spotlight swept across the water behind them.

"Not for long," Sam replied, directing Cade toward a narrow channel between coral formations—a passage that appeared on their navigation system but required local knowledge to navigate safely.

As they entered the channel, the larger pursuit vessel hesitated, unwilling to risk its hull in the shallow passage. Its spotlight continued to sweep the water, but the clustering of local boats and the multiple decoy signatures had created sufficient confusion.

"We've bought some time," Sam noted as they emerged from the channel into the waters near Oistins. "But we need to move quickly once we dock."

The small fishing town's lights provided both navigation aid and operational challenge—visibility meant potential recognition. As Cade guided their boat toward a specific dock on the eastern edge of the harbor, Sam prepared the family for their next moves.

"We'll separate briefly for security," he explained. "Danielle, take Mackie and Rae to the meeting point via the market. Ellie, you and Cade escort Dr. Waters to the secondary location. I'll ensure our pursuers focus on me."

"Divide their attention," Danielle summarized, understanding the strategy—a familiar concept from years of theoretical briefings now applied in real-world conditions.

"Exactly," Sam confirmed. "Twenty minutes, then convergence at the extraction point."

As they docked, the family moved with practiced efficiency despite never having performed this precise operation before. Their individual talents combined with Sam's guidance created a natural operational rhythm. Rae and Mackie followed Danielle toward the busy fish market while Ellie and Cade escorted Coraline in another direction, each group appearing as typical tourists enjoying the local night scene.

Sam remained briefly with the boat, ensuring their equipment was sanitized of identifying information before heading in a third direction—deliberately visible enough to draw attention from potential observers while the others moved undetected through the crowds.

The Friday night Oistins Fish Fry provided perfect operational cover—hundreds of tourists and locals mingling around food stalls, music creating audio coverage, movement and activity masking deliberate patterns. Sam navigated through the market, detecting and confirming surveillance from two of the men he'd observed earlier.

Their focus on him confirmed the effectiveness of the family's separation strategy. Sam led his followers through a predetermined route designed to maximize their distance from the actual extraction point while appearing to be making evasive movements.

Meanwhile, Danielle guided Rae and Mackie through the market with casual purpose, her instructions disguised as tourist enthusiasm.

"The grilled mahi-mahi smells amazing," she commented, steering them toward a specific food stall. "Let's get some before we meet your father."

The vendor recognized the code phrase immediately, nodding toward a narrow alley behind his stall. "Fresh catch just came in. Special preparation around back."

Danielle guided the children through the passage to where a nondescript van waited, its driver a local contact arranged through Flynn's network. Without ceremony, they entered the vehicle and departed, the entire transition taking less than thirty seconds.

Across the market, Ellie and Cade used different methods to ensure Coraline's safety, employing their university students' persona to blend with younger tourists while maintaining situational awareness that belied their age. When they reached their designated connection point—a small dive shop with a back office—the proprietor welcomed them with professional courtesy.

"Equipment rental?" he asked, the standard greeting serving as authentication.

"Night diving certification," Cade replied with the correct countersign.

The shop owner locked the front door, flipping the sign to "Closed" before leading them through the back to another waiting vehicle. Within minutes, both family groups were converging on the extraction point—a private airstrip outside town where a small chartered plane awaited.

Sam's arrival completed the operation, his surveillance evasion successful through a series of calculated misdirections in the town's narrow streets. As the family boarded the aircraft with Coraline, Sam performed a final security check before joining them.

"Nicely executed," he commented as the plane taxied for takeoff. "Everyone followed their instructions perfectly."

"It felt almost natural," Ellie observed, the realization both troubling and satisfying.

"Because it was," Danielle replied, understanding dawning in her expression as she looked at Sam. "That's what we've been doing all along, isn't it? Not just through this trip, but for years."

Sam met her eyes, knowing the time for partial truths had passed. "Every bedtime story about observation games, every family trip with map-reading exercises, every multilingual dinner conversation, every problem-solving challenge. We've been training them their entire lives—even through our difficulties."

The implications settled over the family as the plane lifted into the night sky, leaving the lights of Barbados behind. What had begun as a simple family vacation had crystallized into something far more significant—the revelation of their collective purpose and inherited capabilities.

"Will we go home now?" Mackie asked, his adolescent voice holding both curiosity and uncertainty.

"Yes," Sam answered, meeting each family member's eyes in turn. "But home will never be quite the same."

As the aircraft banked north toward the distant American mainland, the Caribbean Sea stretched below them like a vast dark canvas punctuated by island lights. Somewhere in those waters, manipulated data continued flowing through compromised monitoring stations, part of a global pattern they'd only begun to understand.

The Caribbean cipher had been broken, but the larger code remained to be solved—one that would ultimately require the unique talents of the entire Clayton family, perhaps finally healing the fracture that had defined them for a decade.

Chapter 5
Raleigh Revisited
October 2022

Sam pressed the accelerator of the rented Jeep Compass as they wound through the lush North Carolina countryside, golden autumn leaves spiraling in their wake. Danielle sat beside him, fingers tapping a rhythm on her thigh - her tell when analyzing a situation. The radio played low, masking their conversation from potential surveillance devices.

"Melissa has no idea this isn't just a birthday celebration, does she?" Danielle asked, her voice carrying that blend of experienced insight and vigilance that had evolved significantly since their confrontation in Paris three years earlier.

"Flynn knows. Melissa suspects," Sam replied, eyes scanning the road with practiced vigilance. "They've been married twenty-five years. She notices patterns."

Danielle laughed softly. "Like someone else you know."

The corner of Sam's mouth lifted in acknowledgment. The Paris confrontation had been another turning point in their complex relationship - Danielle demanding full access after years of limited information, her insistence on partnership rather than protection. The gradual thawing that had begun since those traumatic revelations in 2011 had accelerated after Paris. Now here they were, driving toward another family gathering doubling as an intelligence operation, their relationship stronger than it had been in years.

"Flynn sent a message through the secure channel. Alexander's company has new investors." Sam kept his voice neutral, but Danielle immediately understood the implications.

"Consortium connections?"

"Possibly. That's part of why we're here." He tightened his grip on the steering wheel. "Flynn's research team identified anomalies in climate data sets being used by governmental agencies to determine resource allocation."

Danielle gazed out the window at the Research Triangle Park buildings gleaming in the distance. "Just like Copenhagen."

"Just like Copenhagen," Sam confirmed. "But with thirteen years of technological advancement making the manipulation more sophisticated."

The tension between them had transformed over the years - from the raw betrayal and anger of 2011 to the operational synergy they now shared. Since their Paris confrontation, Danielle had moved beyond her limited operational knowledge to become more deeply integrated into Sam's intelligence world, her scientific precision and emotional intelligence becoming invaluable assets in their shared mission.

"The kids know we're checking on Cade's application to NC State's summer program, right?" Danielle's voice lifted, switching to their cover story with the practiced ease of someone who'd been maintaining dual realities for over a decade.

"Among other things. It's a legitimate visit - Melissa's fiftieth, exploring college options. Nothing suspicious about parents looking ahead." Sam took the exit toward Raleigh's suburban sprawl. "Ellie's already getting her environmental science degree up north, but having family at multiple universities creates mobility options."

Danielle nodded. At twenty, Ellie was thriving in her environmental studies program, while eighteen-year-old Rae was exploring linguistics with uncanny aptitude. Sixteen-year-old Cade's programming talents had blossomed into something remarkable - capabilities that made Sam both proud and concerned. And twelve-year-old Mackie's spatial awareness continued developing in ways that reminded Sam uncomfortably of his own youth.

The Clayton children were becoming exactly what Carmichael had predicted. Exactly what made them valuable targets.

Flynn Evans' colonial-style home sat on two acres of wooded property, strategically positioned with clear sightlines and multiple exit routes. As Sam pulled into the circular driveway, he spotted the security cameras disguised as decorative fixtures - newer models than his last visit.

The front door opened before they reached it. Flynn stood there, trim and athletic at fifty-five, his military bearing disguised beneath casual clothes and an easy smile that didn't quite reach his eyes.

"The wanderers return," Flynn called out, enveloping Danielle in a warm hug before clasping Sam's hand with significant pressure - their old signal that secure conversation would come later.

Melissa appeared behind him, elegant at fifty with her dark hair cut in a sophisticated bob. "Finally! I was beginning to think you'd gotten lost somewhere between New York and North Carolina."

"Flight delays," Sam offered smoothly. "The connecting flight through Philadelphia was running behind."

The practiced lie rolled easily off his tongue. They had indeed flown into Raleigh-Durham International, but the extra three hours had been spent in surveillance detection routes and security measures that had become second nature over decades of operational protocol.

Inside, the house hummed with birthday preparation energy. Photographs of Alexander and James - now twenty-six and twenty-two - adorned the walls alongside family vacation memories. Sam noted the new security system panel near the kitchen, disguised as a smart home control.

"Alexander sends his regrets," Melissa said as they settled in the sunroom with coffee. "Some crisis at work he couldn't get away from. James will be here tonight, though."

Sam caught Flynn's fleeting glance. Alexander's absence wasn't coincidental.

"What's keeping Alexander so busy these days?" Danielle asked with perfect casualness, stirring cream into her coffee.

"Cutting-edge stuff," Melissa replied proudly. "His environmental monitoring company just secured major funding. They're developing systems for urban resource management - water, primarily."

"Water management?" Sam kept his tone conversational. "Fascinating field."

"He's thriving," Melissa continued. "Though I hardly understand what he does. Something about predictive modeling for water infrastructure based on climate projections."

Flynn set down his coffee cup with deliberate care. "Sam, I've got that book on the Adirondack watersheds you were asking about. In my office."

The casual invitation was anything but. Sam nodded, squeezing Danielle's shoulder as he stood - their signal that operational information was forthcoming.

Flynn's office occupied the converted sunporch at the back of the house. Once inside, Flynn engaged a signal jammer disguised as a white noise machine for sleep therapy.

"We have twenty minutes before it seems suspicious," Flynn said, his voice dropping to operational clarity. "Alexander doesn't know what his company is actually doing."

"Which is?"

"Developing infrastructure based on manipulated climate projections." Flynn pulled out a tablet, tapping rapidly. "His company, AquaSmart Solutions, received thirty million in funding three months ago from a venture capital firm called Meridian Investments."

"Kessler," Sam stated rather than asked.

"Three shell companies removed, but yes." Flynn displayed a complex organizational chart. "Alexander's technology is legitimate - brilliant, actually. But the data sets they're using for predictive modeling have been subtly altered."

"Creating artificial scarcity where none exists," Sam concluded, the Copenhagen pattern emerging again. "And Alexander has no idea."

"None. He believes he's helping design sustainable water infrastructure." Flynn's face tightened with concern. "The investment gives them access to his technology and algorithms while feeding him manipulated data."

Sam studied the chart, seeing the now-familiar pattern of Consortium operations - legitimate businesses unwittingly advancing their resource control agenda through manipulated climate data.

"There's more," Flynn continued, pulling up a secure file. "Your mother-in-law's humanitarian work in Ukraine has intersected with Consortium interests."

Sam's head snapped up. "Maria? How?"

"Her relief organization has been documenting water access issues in eastern Ukraine. Officially it's conflict-related infrastructure damage, but the pattern matches Consortium manipulation."

"Does she know?"

"Not explicitly, but she's raised questions about inconsistencies in official water quality reports."

Flynn lowered his voice further. "Sam, I think Maria has intelligence connections we weren't aware of."

Sam absorbed this, thinking of Danielle's mother - sophisticated, multilingual Maria Rossi, whose museum curatorship and humanitarian work had taken her across Europe for decades. The possibility had crossed his mind before, especially given Carmichael's cryptic comments about Danielle's family. But confirmation was another matter entirely.

"Does Danielle know?"

"About her mother? I doubt it. Maria's operational security appears exceptional."

The pieces shifted in Sam's mental framework - Danielle's natural aptitude for operational thinking, her family's international connections, her mother's convenient access to conflict zones under cultural pretexts.

"We should bring Cade in," Sam said suddenly, surprising himself.

Flynn raised an eyebrow. "He's sixteen."

"And he's developed an encryption algorithm that might help us identify patterns in the manipulated data sets." Sam held Flynn's gaze. "The Consortium is already targeting him whether he's involved or not. We've confirmed surveillance at his school."

Flynn considered this, then nodded slowly. "Like father, like son."

"But with better preparation than I had," Sam added firmly. "Controlled involvement is safer than ignorance at this point."

The white noise machine beeped once - fifteen minutes elapsed.

"One more thing," Flynn said, pulling up a final document. "Kessler Global Consulting just hired a new Director of Strategic Resources - Ivan Roshkov."

Sam stared at the name, memories of Copenhagen flooding back. The Russian operative who had both warned and threatened him thirteen years ago was now openly working for Kessler.

"Roshkov plays a deeper game than either side fully understands," Sam murmured, echoing Marcus's words from years earlier.

Flynn nodded. "The question is which side he's really on."

Dinner at The Pit Authentic Barbecue downtown was Melissa's birthday choice - a restaurant famous enough to explain their presence while public enough to deter sensitive conversations. James Evans joined them, now a broad-shouldered young man of twenty-two with Flynn's analytical eyes and Melissa's charm.

"Uncle Sam," James greeted him with their old joke, "still teaching kids about rocks and weather?"

"Someone has to," Sam replied with a genuine smile. He'd always enjoyed James's company, watching him grow from a science-obsessed child into a thoughtful entrepreneur who had recently opened a craft brewery.

"How's the beer business?" Danielle asked as they settled into their booth.

"Expanding," James grinned. "Just signed a distribution deal for three states. The warehouse space is massive compared to where we started."

Flynn gave Sam a subtle nod. James's brewery had potential operational value - legitimate business traffic, warehouse space, distribution networks crossing state lines. The Evans family connections were evolving in unexpected ways.

As dinner progressed, Sam's phone buzzed with a secure message from Cade: "Finished preliminary analysis of the data sets Flynn sent. Identified 94% probability of systemic manipulation in eastern Ukrainian water quality assessments. Sending encryption key separately."

Sam felt a complex mixture of pride and concern. Cade's analytical capabilities were extraordinary, but each step deeper into this world put him more firmly on the Consortium's radar.

"Everything okay?" Danielle asked quietly, noting his expression.

"Cade found something," he murmured, angling the phone so she could see.

Her eyes widened slightly before her face returned to pleasant dinner conversation mode. "We should call the kids later to check in. Ellie mentioned helping Rae with her linguistics paper."

The casual comment was their established code for increased family security protocols. Sam nodded, impressed again by how naturally Danielle had adapted to operational communication over the years since that traumatic discovery in 2011.

As the dessert plates arrived with a glowing candle for Melissa, Sam noticed a man at the bar - average height, unremarkable features, attention too carefully directed away from their table. The slight bulge under his sports jacket suggested a shoulder holster.

"Flynn," Sam said casually, "remember that running trail you mentioned? The one around the lake?"

Flynn followed Sam's gaze, registering the surveillance with trained nonchalance. "Umstead State Park. We should go tomorrow morning. Beautiful this time of year."

The coded response confirmed Flynn had identified the tail. Not immediate danger, but a concerning development.

Sam's phone vibrated again with an encrypted message - not from Cade this time, but from a secure channel Sam hadn't used in months. The text contained a single line: "Venice Sphere components identified in eastern Europe. K knows Maria is looking."

A chill ran through Sam's body. The Venice Sphere - the comprehensive data package Marcus had mentioned containing evidence of the Consortium's global operations. And now Maria was somehow involved, perhaps unknowingly.

Melissa blew out her candles to applause, her wish hanging in the air amid the restaurant's cheerful noise. Sam met Danielle's eyes across the table, seeing the silent question there. Later, his slight nod promised. When we're secure.

The family dynamics around the table carried on with practiced normalcy - birthday celebrations, college discussions, brewery business. Beneath it all, the currents of something much larger flowed, connecting Copenhagen to Paris to Barbados to this moment in Raleigh.

Sam watched James describing his distribution routes with animated gestures, thinking how easily the brewery's legitimate commerce could provide cover for intelligence movement. He saw Flynn's careful attention to their surroundings, Melissa's perceptive gaze noting the subtle shifts in conversation, Danielle's seamless integration of operational awareness with genuine family affection - a skill she had perfected through years of maintaining a functional co-parenting relationship despite the emotional distance that had lingered since their 2011 crisis.

The compartmentalization that had dominated their marriage for so long was dissolving, not through

"Intelligence affiliated," Flynn confirmed gently. "Has been for decades, from what we can gather. Cultural and humanitarian access providing intelligence collection opportunities."

Danielle absorbed this, her expression shifting from shock to a kind of recognition. "The galleries. The museum connections. Her language skills..." She shook her head slowly. "I always thought she was just naturally talented with people and languages."

"She is," Sam said, taking Danielle's hand. "That's often why people are recruited."

"Like our children," Danielle said quietly, the implication hanging between them.

The silence stretched, filled only with birdsong and distant hiking voices.

"We need to coordinate with Maria," Sam finally said. "Whether she acknowledges her affiliation or not, she's identified Consortium activity in Ukraine that connects to what we found in Barbados and what Flynn's team discovered here."

"And we need to protect Alexander," Flynn added grimly. "He's unwittingly developing technology that furthers their agenda."

Danielle squared her shoulders, processing the revelation about her mother with remarkable composure. "We need Cade's algorithm to verify the connection between these manipulated data sets."

Sam nodded, pride mixing with parental concern. "I'll set up a secure communication protocol. Limited information, carefully compartmentalized."

Flynn gave Sam a significant look. "The compartmentalization you've maintained isn't sustainable anymore, Sam. Not with the Consortium targeting family connections directly."

The words echoed what Danielle had been saying since Paris, what Sam had been gradually accepting in the years since the East Coast trek revealed both his secret life and the surveillance focused on their children.

"They're still just our children," Danielle said firmly. "Not assets or packages or capabilities."

"Of course," Flynn agreed quickly. "But they've inherited certain... aptitudes that make them valuable. And vulnerable."

Sam thought of Cade's remarkable programming skills, Rae's linguistic facility, Ellie's environmental insights, even young Mackie's spatial awareness.

Talents that had seemed like fortunate genetic gifts now appeared as inherited operational capabilities - exactly what Carmichael had hinted at.

"We protect them by preparing them," Sam said, meeting Danielle's gaze. "It's all we can do."

"Then we prepare them together," she replied. "No more separate worlds."

The phrase had been their mantra since Paris - a continuation of the journey that began with that traumatic discovery in 2011. No more separate worlds. No more partial truths. A true partnership forged through crisis and commitment.

As they walked back toward the parking area, Sam's secure phone vibrated with an incoming message. The sender ID made his breath catch - a channel he hadn't seen active in years.

"Marcus?" Danielle asked, reading his expression.

Sam nodded, opening the encrypted message: "Roshkov position confirmed. Double operation in progress. Venice Sphere components scattered as insurance. Maria holds key fragment unwittingly. Extraction protocol Midnight Saxophone initiated."

"He's alive," Sam whispered, hope and disbelief mingling.

Flynn's eyebrows rose. "Marcus Cartier? That's not possible. The Brussels incident was confirmed."

"Apparently not confirmed enough," Sam said, showing him the message authentication code only Marcus would know.

Flynn studied it, professional skepticism warring with the evidence. "If he's alive, and initiating Midnight Saxophone..."

"Then this is bigger than we thought," Sam finished.

The implications rippled outward. Marcus alive. Maria involved. The Venice Sphere scattered as insurance against Consortium action. And most concerning - Roshkov operating as a double agent within Kessler's organization.

As they reached the parking area, a jogger passed them on the trail - ordinary enough except for the momentary eye contact with Sam that lasted a beat too long. The slight nod was almost imperceptible.

Contact protocol established. The operative would approach later when secure.

Flynn caught the exchange, his hand instinctively moving toward his concealed weapon before Sam's subtle head shake stopped him.

"The most effective security is what they don't expect," Flynn murmured, echoing their old training principle.

"And what they don't expect," Sam replied, watching the jogger disappear around the bend, "is that we're no longer operating alone."

Danielle slipped her arm through Sam's as they walked to the car, the gesture both affectionate and supportive - a reflection of how far they'd come from the devastating betrayal of 2011. "So what happens now?"

Sam thought of Cade's message, of Maria's unknowing involvement, of Alexander's compromised company, of Marcus somehow alive and orchestrating from the shadows.

"Now," he said, "we adapt."

Later that evening, in the quiet security of Flynn's home office, Sam initiated a carefully encrypted video call to Cade. The specialized software Cade had developed himself routed the connection through seventeen different nodes, making it virtually untraceable.

Cade's face appeared on the screen, his blonde curls falling across his forehead as he leaned forward. At sixteen, his features were maturing into a blend of Sam and Danielle, but his intense focus was entirely his own.

"Dad, you got my analysis?" he asked without preamble.

"I did. Extraordinary work," Sam replied, studying his son's expression. This conversation would cross a line - bringing Cade directly into operational awareness rather than keeping him on the periphery with plausible deniability.

"The data manipulation is sophisticated," Cade continued, his fingers flying across his keyboard. "But there's a pattern signature I've isolated. Look at this."

The screen split to show a complex visualization of data points - climate measurements across multiple regions with subtle anomalies highlighted.

"The manipulations aren't random," Cade explained, his voice taking on the precise tone he used when solving complex problems. "They follow a mathematical pattern that creates artificial trends when processed through standard climate modeling algorithms."

Sam watched his son's analysis with a mixture of pride and concern. "And you developed this detection method yourself?"

"Based on that encryption concept we discussed last year," Cade nodded. "Remember when we were talking about prime number applications in cryptography? I adapted it to look for artificially constructed data patterns."

Danielle moved into frame beside Sam, her expression warm but serious. "Cade, what you've found is important. More important than you might realize."

Cade's eyes shifted between them, intelligence sharpening his gaze. "This isn't just about NC State's summer program, is it?"

The moment stretched between them - the precipice between the childhood they'd tried to preserve and the reality they could no longer shield him from.

"No," Sam admitted finally. "It's about something much larger. Something that affects our family directly."

Cade nodded slowly, unsurprised. "The surveillance at school. The security protocols at home. The 'vacations' that always seem to include educational side trips to very specific locations." A small, knowing smile touched his lips. "I'm not exactly an average teenager, Dad."

"No," Sam agreed quietly. "You never have been."

"None of you have," Danielle added. "But that doesn't mean you shouldn't have normal experiences."

Cade's expression grew serious. "Is this why you've been teaching me encryption techniques since I was twelve? Why we have all those 'emergency drills' at home?"

Sam and Danielle exchanged glances, a lifetime of shared decisions passing between them.

"Yes," Sam answered simply. "There are people interested in our family because of certain... capabilities we seem to have inherited."

"The pattern recognition," Cade said immediately. "The way we all seem to notice things others don't."

"Among other things," Danielle confirmed.

Cade absorbed this, his analytical mind visibly processing implications. "Ellie's environmental insights. Rae's language abilities. My programming. Even Mackie's spatial visualization."

"All valuable skills," Sam said carefully. "Skills that certain organizations would very much like to control or exploit."

Understanding dawned in Cade's eyes. "That's why someone tried to separate me from you at the Smithsonian when I was four."

The memory of that moment - the operative attempting to isolate Cade using a museum security uniform as cover - still sent ice through Sam's veins. "You remember that?"

"Not clearly," Cade admitted. "But I remember being frightened, then you appearing suddenly, and then our vacation plans changing."

Sam nodded. "That was the first direct attempt. There have been others - surveillance mostly, but occasionally more direct approaches."

"And now?" Cade asked, his voice steady despite the revelations.

"Now we need your help," Sam said simply. "Your algorithm has identified something critical - evidence of deliberate manipulation of climate data that's being used to control water resources globally."

Cade's eyes widened slightly, the programmer in him immediately grasping the implications. "You're talking about weaponized data. Creating artificial shortages through manipulated projections."

"Exactly," Danielle confirmed. "And your algorithm provides the first concrete evidence linking different operations across multiple continents."

"Who's doing this?" Cade asked.

"A group we call the Consortium," Sam explained. "Powerful interests using climate data manipulation to control resources and markets."

Cade nodded slowly, piecing things together. "And our family is somehow involved in opposing them."

It wasn't a question. Sam's chest tightened with a father's pride mixed with profound concern. "Yes. For many years now."

"Since before we were born," Cade concluded, the brilliant analytical mind that made him both gifted and vulnerable working through the timeline. "That's why we have all these 'family traditions' that double as security protocols."

Sam smiled slightly. "We've been training you your entire lives. We just didn't want you to know that's what we were doing."

"Until now," Cade said, understanding dawning. "Because the danger exists whether I'm aware of it or not."

"The danger exists regardless," Sam confirmed. "The difference is now you're prepared."

Cade was quiet for a moment, absorbing the magnitude of what they'd shared. Then his fingers returned to the keyboard, bringing up another data visualization.

"If what you're saying is true, then this pattern I found isn't just academic," he said, highlighting a section of the analysis. "It's evidence of systematic resource manipulation across multiple regions."

"It is," Danielle confirmed.

"Then I want to help," Cade said simply. "Tell me what you need."

The conversation continued for almost an hour - carefully controlled information, specific technical requests, security protocols established. Sam watched his son transition from gifted teenager to operational asset before his eyes, the inherited capabilities that had always been present now finding focused purpose.

When they finally disconnected, Sam sat back in Flynn's office chair, emotions churning beneath his composed exterior.

"We did the right thing," Danielle said softly, reading his thoughts as she so often did.

"I hope so," Sam replied. "I've spent their entire lives trying to keep them separate from this world."

"Their abilities were always there," Danielle reminded him. "This just gives them purpose."

Flynn knocked softly before entering, closing the door behind him. "How did Cade take it?"

"Like he'd been waiting for this conversation his whole life," Sam admitted.

Flynn nodded. "In some ways, he probably has been. The patterns were there for someone as observant as he is."

"The Consortium has already identified him as a person of interest," Sam said, the operational reality settling heavily. "At least now he understands the security protocols."

"Limited information," Danielle emphasized. "Technical support only, not field operations."

"For now," Flynn acknowledged. "Though at sixteen, he's already more knowledgeable than many analysts I work with."

The secure phone buzzed with an incoming message - the jogger from the park making contact. Sam read the brief text, his expression hardening.

"Maria's position has been compromised," he stated flatly. "Ukrainian intelligence reports Consortium operatives moving into position near her humanitarian mission."

"We need to warn her," Danielle said immediately.

"Already done," Flynn replied, checking his own secure device. "Extraction team en route from Poland. Twelve hours at most."

Sam processed this, mentally calculating contingencies. "And Alexander?"

"James is bringing him to the brewery tonight under the pretense of birthday celebrations," Flynn explained. "We'll brief him there. Secure location, no electronic devices, plausible reason for family gathering."

The pieces were moving faster now, connections between Copenhagen, Paris, Barbados, and Raleigh forming a pattern as clear as any Cade had identified in his data analysis. The Consortium's global manipulation of climate data for resource control, the targeted interest in families with specific inherited capabilities, the Venice Sphere containing comprehensive evidence scattered across continents.

"Midnight Saxophone," Sam murmured, thinking of Marcus's extraction protocol code. "Carmichael's composition. The one he recorded in 1983."

"What's the significance?" Flynn asked.

"The music continues between the notes," Sam quoted, the phrase Carmichael had used, that Roshkov had repeated in Copenhagen, that had appeared again in the saxophone reed encryption from Carmichael's case.

Understanding dawned in Danielle's eyes. "The spaces between the notes in that composition - they're a code, aren't they?"

Sam nodded. "Coordinates. Extraction points. Safe houses." He looked at Flynn with renewed purpose. "We need to get Maria out, protect Alexander, and secure Cade's algorithm."

"And then?" Danielle asked.

"Then we follow the music," Sam replied. "Note by note, until we find all the pieces of the Venice Sphere."

As evening settled over Raleigh, the operational tempo increased. Security measures implemented, extraction coordinates transmitted, family protections established. Through it all, Sam felt the familiar weight of responsibility - now expanded beyond his own operational security to encompass the family he had spent decades trying to shield.

Yet alongside that weight was a new sensation - the strength of shared purpose. Danielle's steady presence. Flynn's operational expertise. Cade's remarkable capabilities. Maria's unexpected connection. Even James's brewery offering strategic value.

As they prepared to leave the office, Flynn placed a hand on Sam's shoulder. "The protocols are sound, but remember – the most effective security is what they don't expect." As Sam drove back to the hotel later, his mind kept returning to the earlier video call with Carmichael. His father had seemed distracted, repeating a story he'd told just days before. Little things like this had been happening more frequently—momentary confusion, searching for words that once came easily. Sam tried to dismiss it as simple fatigue or age, but something about the pattern troubled him deeply.

The compartmentalization was ending, not through compromise but through integration. Family and duty no longer separated by impermeable walls but now flowing together in currents of shared purpose - a journey that had begun with that painful discovery in 2011 and was now approaching something like reconciliation.

As they prepared for the brewery meeting that would bring Alexander into awareness, Sam thought of his children - each developing in ways Carmichael had somehow anticipated, each vulnerable and valuable because of the very talents that made them exceptional.

"They're creating a complete environmental surveillance network disguised as climate research," Cade had said during their video call, seeing the pattern in the manipulated data. "The perfect information advantage. They see the real data while everyone else acts on the manipulated predictions."

His son's words echoed in Sam's mind as they drove through the darkening Raleigh streets toward James's brewery. The perfect information advantage - exactly what the Consortium had been building for decades. Exactly what the Venice Sphere would expose.

And now, Sam reflected as the brewery came into view, his family was fully part of that exposure. Not as targets, but as active participants in their own protection.

The music continued between the notes, linking past to present, Copenhagen to Raleigh, Carmichael to Sam to Cade. A composition spanning generations, moving toward its crescendo.

By this time back home, subtle changes in Carmichael had begun to surface—initially easy enough for Sam to dismiss as simple aging or stress. Missed details in conversations, repeating anecdotes he'd shared only days before, occasional hesitations that felt out of character for the usually meticulous man. Sam initially attributed it to fatigue, a passing fog soon to clear. But as months unfolded, the signs grew undeniable, a quiet shadow settling over the sharp edges of Carmichael's once-formidable mind.

Chapter 6
Italian Anniversary
July 2024

Sunlight spilled across the rooftops of Castelpetroso, bathing the small Italian village in golden light. Sam Clayton stood on the balcony of their hotel room, watching the morning light play across the distant hills toward Frosolone. The morning air carried the scent of fresh bread and coffee from the café below, mingling with the distinctive aroma of a countryside that had witnessed millennia of secrets.

"You know Carmichael would've loved this place, years ago—back when his mind was still sharp," Danielle said, joining him at the railing, her gaze lingering thoughtfully before settling on Sam.

"I know. It feels strange being here, celebrating, while he's slipping further away. But he'd hate us sitting idle, trapped in his fog," Sam replied, his eyes tracking the movement of a vintage Fiat winding its way along the narrow road below.

Danielle reached across, gently touching his hand. "He'd tell you the fight goes on. That sometimes stepping away, even briefly, is how you find clarity to fight harder."

Sam exhaled slowly, letting her words settle over him as he glanced toward the distant hills. Shaking off the melancholy, he squeezed her hand lightly and forced a smile. "Alright," he said softly. "Let's at least try to enjoy this."

As sunlight dappled the ancient stone facade, Sam watched his wife arrange her chestnut curls in the reflection of an antique mirror. Thirty years of marriage had only deepened the quiet grace in her movements, the enduring affection in her warm brown eyes.

"Happy anniversary," he said, crossing the room to slip his arms around her waist.

Danielle turned in his embrace, studying his face with the perceptive gaze that had become more knowing with each passing year. "Thirty years. Who would have thought that awkward earth science teacher would turn out to be such a good investment?"

"I believe your exact words were 'promising but needs work,'" Sam replied, the corners of his green eyes crinkling. The morning light caught the silver strands at his temples, evidence of the years between them and the young couple who'd exchanged vows in that small church in West Chazy.

She brushed her fingers across his cheek, her expression shifting to something more serious. "This isn't just an anniversary trip, is it, Sam?"

The question hung between them, loaded with the weight of their history. Since Paris five years ago, since Barbados, since Raleigh, they had been rebuilding what fractured that day in 2011. Danielle had moved from operational awareness to partnership, but the emotional distance had been slower to heal.

"No," he admitted, taking her hands in his. "It's not just an anniversary trip."

Her fingers tightened around his. "Then tell me everything. No more walls between us, remember?"

"The Rossi family records. Your cousins in Frosolone. There's a connection to what I've been tracking—what we've been tracking—since Copenhagen." The words came easier now than they once had, the practice of sharing becoming more natural with time. "Climate data manipulation, resource control, the Consortium—it all connects to records that may have been preserved through your family."

Danielle nodded, her expression revealing a confidence born of years of involvement rather than surprise. "I've wondered about that. The way my mother's side has always kept those old family records, the museum work, the restoration projects..." She paused, a half-smile forming. "We've come a long way since our East Coast Trek, haven't we?"

Sam's expression softened at the reference to their darkest moment thirteen years ago, when his secret life had shattered their marriage. "We have."

"I want this to be different, Sam," she continued, her eyes meeting his directly. "Not just an operational partnership. I want us—really us—back. After all these years of working alongside each other but still keeping that emotional distance..."

The burner phone on the nightstand buzzed, interrupting the moment with its harsh electronic tone. Sam checked the message, his expression tightening almost imperceptibly.

"Contact confirmed," he said, locking eyes with his wife. "We'll meet your cousin Riccardo in two hours."

The Alfa Romeo Stelvio handled the winding roads with precision, hugging each curve as they ascended into the hills surrounding Frosolone. Sam drove with casual expertise, one hand resting lightly on the wheel while his eyes continuously scanned their surroundings. The dark gray vehicle blended with the shadows cast by ancient olive trees lining the narrow road.

"You're doing it again," Danielle observed, her tone gently teasing as she looked up from the old family photograph album in her lap.

"Doing what?"

"The thing with your eyes. Establishing baseline, identifying potential blind spots, mapping escape routes." She smiled at his surprised expression. "I've been watching you do this for thirteen years, Sam. Ever since I found out."

He chuckled, the tension in his shoulders easing slightly. "Makes me wonder what else you've noticed."

"More than you think," she replied, her gaze returning to the album. "Like how this family tree has some interesting inconsistencies. My great-uncle Giovanni is listed, but with conspicuous gaps in his timeline—listed as 'traveling' from 1962 to 1971 with almost no details, then reappearing briefly at my parents' wedding. The records of his activities are suspiciously incomplete. Then there's my mother's unexplained 'art fellowship' in Vienna during the height of the Cold War."

The question hung between them—seemingly innocent yet hovering at the edge of territories Sam had spent decades keeping separate. Was this the moment to begin bridging his compartmentalized lives, as Carmichael had advised? Or was protective distance still the safest approach?

"He was a complicated man," Sam answered carefully. "Much of his life remained private, even from family."

"Like father, like son?" Danielle's smile softened the observation, but her eyes—so much like her mother's—missed nothing.

Sam felt a familiar tension—the operative's instinct for security wrestling with a husband's desire for honesty. Throughout decades of living divided lives, Sam had always felt pulled between competing purposes.

The small town square of Frosolone seemed frozen in time, its ancient church and stone buildings bathed in the harsh midday sun. A handful of old men played cards at a café table, while a few tourists snapped photos of the picturesque mountain views. Sam parked the Alfa Romeo in a small lot behind the church, his movements casual yet precise as he scanned for surveillance.

"Where will we meet Riccardo?" Danielle asked, smoothing her linen dress as they walked toward Piazza Municipio.

"He's expecting us here," Sam replied, guiding her toward a small café nestled in the corner of the square. "He said he'd approach us."

The café was cool and dim after the brightness outside, stone walls and heavy wooden beams creating a sanctuary from the summer heat. A tall man with olive skin and Danielle's same warm brown eyes rose from a corner table as they entered. The family resemblance was unmistakable—the same elegant profile that Sam had admired in his wife for three decades.

"Cugina Danielle," he said, embracing her warmly before extending a hand to Sam. "And Professor Clayton. Benvenuti a Frosolone."

"Grazie, Riccardo," Danielle replied in fluent Italian, the language of her grandfather, Giuseppe, flowing naturally. "È passato troppo tempo."

They settled at the table, the casual appearance of a family reunion masking the tension beneath the surface. A waiter brought espresso and mineral water without being asked, then retreated to the back room.

"The café is secure," Riccardo said in perfect English, his voice low. "Paolo is family. Three generations of Rossis have had important conversations at this table."

"Including conversations about climate data going back to the 1960s?" Sam asked quietly.

Riccardo's eyes narrowed slightly, evaluating Sam with newfound interest. "So it's true, then. Maria said you were involved, but I wasn't certain how deeply." He leaned forward, lowering his voice further. "The Consortium has been manipulating environmental data for decades. My work as a veterinarian gives me access to agricultural records, animal health statistics across southern Italy. The patterns are there if you know how to look."

"My mother knew about this?" Danielle asked, surprise coloring her voice.

"Maria has been tracking resource manipulation patterns since before you were born," Riccardo confirmed, his expression softening at Danielle's obvious shock. "The museum work, the art authentication—all covers for monitoring document manipulation. The Rossi family has a tradition of... alternative service."

"Intelligence work," Sam clarified, watching his wife process this revelation about her family.

"My mother is intelligence?" Danielle repeated, this time with certainty rather than question.

"Not officially, perhaps," Riccardo replied, stirring his espresso. "But the Rossi family has provided assistance to certain agencies for generations. Your grandfather Giuseppe had connections to OSS operations during the war. Your uncle Giovanni worked with NATO intelligence through the Cold War, explaining his mysterious absences. Your mother's specialty became document authentication —a skill particularly valuable when examining historical climate records."

Danielle sat back, a complex mix of emotions crossing her face. "All those summers in New York city, the museum tours, the endless lessons in art history and document preservation..."

"She was training you," Sam said gently, reaching for her hand. "Just as my father trained me, though I didn't recognize it either."

"The music continues between the notes," Riccardo said quietly, watching Sam's reaction.

Sam's head snapped up, green eyes locking onto Riccardo's face. "Carmichael's phrase. How do you know it?"

"Your father's encryption methods became legendary in certain circles," Riccardo explained. "Jazz-based cryptography adapted by European assets throughout the 1970s. And your mother knew about

Sam's connection to Marcus Cartier and kept quiet about it to you."

Danielle looked between them, pieces falling into place. "Our meeting wasn't coincidence, was it? My transfer to SUNY Plattsburgh from Albany when Sam moved back from Amsterdam..."

"Not entirely," Sam admitted, the revelation landing with unexpected weight. "Marcus encouraged me to take the teaching position in Plattsburgh. I always thought it was for operational convenience, being near the Canadian border."

"Families with certain aptitudes tend to find each other," Riccardo said cryptically. "The Claytons and the Rossis have complementary skills. Useful skills."

"So this is an internal power struggle," Sam concluded.

"In part. But my primary allegiance remains as it always has been—to the same entity your father served."

Sam felt Danielle's hand tighten around his. "And what entity is that?"

"One that values balance over dominance." Riccardo checked his watch. "Two minutes remaining. What matters now is this: Kessler will not be at the symposium, but he's directed resources to disrupt it. The evidence you present will be attacked as fraudulent. You need credible, public verification from multiple sources."

As they left the café, Danielle slipped her arm through Sam's, her presence steady beside him. The town square continued its timeless rhythm—old men playing cards, tourists taking photographs, everyday life unfolding in blissful ignorance of the shadows moving beneath the surface.

"You okay?" Sam asked quietly as they walked toward the car.

"Processing," she replied honestly. "Finding out your mother has been intelligence all along changes... well, everything."

"Not everything," Sam countered, squeezing her hand. "It doesn't change who you are, who we are together."

"But it changes how I understand myself," she said thoughtfully. "All those family traditions, the focus on languages, document preservation, observation skills... I thought I was just raised by a detail-oriented museum curator."

"You were raised by a woman who wanted you to have the skills to navigate a complex world," Sam replied. "Just as we've done with our children, though with less awareness on our part."

They reached the Alfa Romeo, and Sam performed a quick security check before unlocking it. As Danielle settled into the passenger seat, she gave him a measured look.

"Our children," she repeated. "Who are developing into quite the remarkable adults, with talents that seem increasingly relevant to our current situation."

Sam nodded, starting the engine. "I've been thinking about that too. Ellie's environmental data analysis, Rae's linguistics, Cade's algorithms, even Mackie's spatial modeling... they're all skills that would be incredibly useful right now."

"They're not children anymore, Sam," Danielle said quietly. "And they've grown up with our security protocols for over a decade now. Since 2011, they've known something was different about our family, even if they didn't know the full extent."

The implication hung between them as Sam navigated the winding road back toward their hotel. The question of their children's involvement had been growing more pressing with each revelation, each crisis. If the Consortium was tracking families with certain aptitudes, as Marcus had warned years ago, then the Clayton children had been on their radar since birth.

"One step at a time," Sam finally said. "Let's see what Lucia has at the museum tomorrow. Then we'll discuss how to handle the children's involvement going forward."

Danielle nodded, seeming satisfied with this approach for now. "Fair enough. But Sam?"

"Yes?"

"When the time comes—and it will—I want them fully integrated, not just partially informed like I was for all those years after our East Coast Trek. What happened in the Smithsonian with Cade all those years ago... I never want any of us vulnerable like that again."

Sam's jaw tightened at the memory of the near-abduction at the Smithsonian, one of the incidents that had forced him to share more with Danielle after their crisis in 2011. "Agreed. We protect them by preparing them. It's all we can do."

"Then we prepare them together," Danielle replied firmly. "No more emotional distance between us. That's what nearly broke us in 2011 and what we've been slowly rebuilding since then."

The hotel room in Castelpetroso felt different when they returned—not just a luxury anniversary accommodation, but an operational base. Sam secured the room methodically, checking for surveillance while Danielle organized the materials from Riccardo.

"I still can't believe my mother never told me," she said, spreading photographs across the bed. "All those years..."

"Compartmentalization," Sam replied, finishing his security sweep. "The same reason I kept things from you, from the children. The belief that separation equals safety."

"Does it?" she asked, looking up from the photographs.

Sam considered the question seriously, thinking of all the near-misses over the years, all the times his family had been at risk despite his efforts to keep them separate from his operational life.

"No," he finally admitted. "I don't think it does. Not anymore. Maybe it never did."

Danielle nodded, accepting his answer without judgment. "I've spent thirteen years in your world, Sam, ever since that day in 2011 when everything fell apart. I've learned the protocols, handled operations, even led the Barbados extraction. But there's always been this... distance between us, even when we were working side by side."

"I know," Sam acknowledged, the weight of unsaid words between them finally lifting. "After you found out, after how badly I hurt you by keeping my life secret... I never thought we'd get back what we lost."

"But we never really lost it, did we?" Danielle asked, moving closer to him. "We just buried it under protocols and operations and necessity."

"And fear," Sam added quietly. "Fear that you could never really forgive me."

"So what's our next move?" Danielle asked, shifting the conversation but holding his gaze with new warmth.

"Naples tomorrow," Sam replied. "We'll go to the archaeological museum with Lucia in the morning.

Then we'll need to evaluate what we find before determining further steps."

"And if we find what we expect? Evidence of the Consortium's manipulation through historical records?"

Sam moved to the window, looking out at the picturesque Italian countryside that concealed centuries of conflict and intrigue beneath its beautiful surface.

"Then we follow the trail wherever it leads. Venice, most likely, based on what Marcus indicated before his disappearance. That's where the central data repository—the Venice Sphere—is supposed to be located."

Danielle joined him at the window, her presence beside him now that of a wife and partner in every sense. The last barriers between them were falling away, revealing a new landscape of possibility—and reconciliation.

"Venice," she repeated thoughtfully. "I've always wanted to see Venice."

"Not like this," Sam warned, knowing the dangers that awaited them.

Danielle's expression remained resolute, her warm brown eyes meeting his without hesitation. "Exactly like this. Together, finally. True partners after all these years."

He nodded, accepting the new reality between them as the Italian sun began its descent toward the ancient hills. Whatever came next—Naples, Venice, the Consortium—they would face it together, the division between them no longer a wall but a bridge.

"No more walls between us," he agreed, taking her hand as the golden light of evening transformed the landscape below. Tomorrow would bring new dangers, new revelations, but for this moment, they stood united in purpose and understanding for perhaps the first time since that fateful day on the East Coast thirteen years ago.

The sun disappeared behind the mountains, casting long shadows across the valley—shadows that seemed to whisper of secrets yet to be uncovered, of connections spanning generations and continents, of a family legacy only beginning to reveal itself, and of a marriage finally healing after years of functional partnership without true emotional reconciliation.

Chapter 7
Naples and Pompeii Shadows
July 2024

Swirling shadows danced across ancient stone as Sam and Danielle ducked into a narrow alley off the main tourist route in Naples. Heart pounding against his ribs, Sam pressed his back against the cool stone wall, pulling Danielle close as footsteps echoed on cobblestones behind them. They had barely escaped the ambush at the archaeological museum, losing their pursuers in the labyrinthine streets of the Spanish Quarter.

"Think we lost them?" Danielle whispered, her breath warm against his neck.

Sam peered around the corner, scanning the bustling street where tourists and locals mingled in the afternoon heat. "For now. But they know we're onto something significant." His fingers tightened around the small thumb drive extracted from the museum's climate records archive—evidence of systematic tampering with historical records dating back centuries.

Danielle's eyes gleamed with determination, her analytical mind already processing their next move. After thirteen years of working operations together —ever since that traumatic discovery on their East Coast Trek—Sam recognized that look. The walls between his compartmentalized lives had finally fallen completely, not just professionally but emotionally.

"We need to understand what connects the Vatican archives to the museum records," she said, her voice steady despite their narrow escape. "And why someone's willing to kill to protect centuries-old climate data."

Sam nodded, checking his watch. "Our contact at Pompeii will be waiting. If anyone can help us make sense of this historical manipulation, it's Alessandra."

As they merged back into the stream of tourists, Sam felt Danielle's hand slip into his—a gesture that once would have been purely practical but now carried the weight of their renewed connection.

Since Paris five years ago, when she'd demanded full access after years of limited information, and especially since their breakthrough in Barbados, they'd been rebuilding what had fractured in 2011. This mission was as much about completing their reconciliation as it was about uncovering the truth.

Professor Alessandra Bianchi waited for them at the entrance to Pompeii, her tall figure easy to spot among the tourist groups. At fifty-seven, she carried herself with the confident posture of someone comfortable in harsh field conditions, her olive skin weathered from years studying Mediterranean volcanoes. Her expertise in historical volcanic activity had made her an unexpected but vital ally— one of the first scientists to notice discrepancies in climate records tied to major eruptions.

"I was concerned when you were late," she said, bypassing pleasantries as she led them through a side entrance away from the main tourist flow. Her voice carried the musical cadence of northern Italian with flawless English vocabulary. "After what happened at the museum, we must assume all official sites are compromised."

"You heard about that already?" Sam asked, surprised at how quickly information had traveled.

Alessandra's expression remained neutral, though her eyes scanned continuously for observers. "When men with diplomatic credentials pursue American tourists through Naples' archaeological museum, certain networks take notice." She handed them visitor badges bearing false names. "Today you are Canadian researchers assisting my volcanic study. It gives us access to restricted areas."

They followed her through the ancient city, past groups of tourists photographing remarkably preserved buildings. Pompeii always struck Sam with its eerie sense of suspended time—a moment of catastrophe frozen for millennia. Today, that preservation felt unnervingly relevant to their mission.

"The manipulation of historical records follows distinct patterns," Alessandra explained as they walked. "Most scientists assumed discrepancies between Byzantine accounts of climate events and physical evidence were simply errors in historical documentation. I began questioning this assumption five years ago when studying tephra layers from Vesuvius."

She led them toward the northeastern section of the ruins, away from the main tourist areas. "What initially appeared as inconsistencies in historical weather accounts suddenly formed patterns when compared across multiple Mediterranean cultures. Records were systematically altered to minimize certain climate events while exaggerating others."

"But why alter records from thousands of years ago?" Danielle asked.

"To establish false baselines," Sam answered, the pattern becoming clear. "Modern climate models rely on historical data for comparison. If you controlled the historical narrative..."

"You could manipulate projections without changing current data," Alessandra finished. "Create artificial patterns that serve your purposes."

Danielle nodded. "It's similar to what we uncovered in the Barbados operation three years ago." She exchanged a meaningful glance with Sam, both remembering their first significant field operation together after years of limited involvement. That mission had marked the beginning of genuine healing between them.

They reached a modest building with a small courtyard, identified by a simple sign as the "House of the Faun." Alessandra nodded to a security guard who unlocked a barrier, allowing them into a section closed to regular tourists.

Inside, the professor led them to a room with remarkably preserved frescoes. "This house contained one of the most comprehensive libraries in ancient Pompeii. When excavated in the 1830s, they discovered remnants of scrolls describing weather patterns and agricultural records."

She lowered her voice. "What few people know is that in 2015, new ground-penetrating radar identified a previously undiscovered room beneath this section. The contents were never publicly cataloged."

Alessandra pressed a section of decorative tiling, revealing a modern keypad disguised within the ancient patterns. After entering a code, a section of flooring slid aside, exposing narrow stairs leading downward.

"The Italian Cultural Ministry classified this area for 'ongoing research.' Only five people have authorization to access it." She gave them a tight smile. "Fortunately, I'm one of them."

As they descended into the cool darkness, Sam felt the weight of history pressing down—not just the physical stone above them, but the centuries of manipulated information they were beginning to uncover. Whatever was hidden here had remained concealed first by volcanic ash, then by deliberate obscurity for two millennia.

The hidden chamber beneath the House of the Faun contained a modern research facility that contrasted sharply with the ancient ruins above. Climate-controlled glass cases housed partially preserved scrolls alongside advanced imaging equipment and computer workstations.

"These documents were found sealed in lead containers, remarkably preserved," Alessandra explained. "They contain detailed weather observations from 120 BCE to 79 CE, the year of Vesuvius' eruption."

She pulled up digital scans on a monitor. "Roman agricultural records were extraordinarily precise about rainfall, temperature patterns, and growing seasons. This data should align with other indicators like tree rings and ice cores."

"But they don't," Danielle stated, studying the translated texts. Her scientific background had proven invaluable throughout their years of operations, allowing her to quickly identify patterns where others might miss them.

"No," Alessandra confirmed. "When I compared these records with official climate databases used for current modeling, I found systematic discrepancies. The official records show a much more stable climate than actually existed."

Sam examined the ancient records. "If these show greater historical climate fluctuations than officially acknowledged..."

"Then modern changes might appear more anomalous than they truly are," Danielle finished. "Creating the impression of unprecedented patterns."

Their synchronized thinking wasn't new—it had developed over thirteen years of operational partnership, even during the times when their personal relationship remained strained. The years of co-parenting while maintaining operational security had forged a unique connection between them, one that had evolved from necessity to genuine partnership.

Alessandra nodded. "Exactly. By minimizing historical variations, current changes seem more dramatic—or less so—depending on what narrative you wish to create."

She pulled up another file on her computer. "This pattern extends beyond Pompeii. My colleagues identified similar inconsistencies in climate records from Egypt, Greece, and Northern Europe."

"Who would have the resources to alter historical records across multiple countries and time periods?" Danielle asked.

"Someone playing a very long game," Sam answered, the scale of the conspiracy coming into focus. "Someone who understood that controlling historical baselines would provide leverage over future resource allocation."

Alessandra's expression grew grave. "The alteration isn't recent. I've traced systematic changes to historical climate records beginning in the late 1950s and accelerating in the following decades."

"The Consortium has been planning this for generations," Sam said quietly.

"Not just planning," Danielle corrected. "Implementing. Layer by layer, decade by decade."

Alessandra handed them a small device resembling an external hard drive. "This contains my complete research, including evidence of tampering with climate records from twenty-three historical archives. I've documented authentication methods that prove the original records were altered in official databases."

Sam pocketed the device. "This could validate everything we've gathered from Copenhagen to Barbados."

"We should examine the Herculaneum records as well," Danielle suggested. "If this pattern holds across multiple preservation sites..."

Alessandra's phone chimed with a museum security alert. She checked the message, her expression darkening. "Someone just accessed the system using my colleague's credentials. He's currently at a conference in Berlin."

Sam immediately moved toward the stairs. "How many ways out of this facility?"

"Just the main entrance and an emergency exit that leads to the maintenance area," Alessandra replied, already shutting down the computer systems.

"Time to use the emergency option," Sam said, helping gather their research materials.

Danielle quickly photographed several key documents with her specialized camera before they followed Alessandra toward a red door marked "Uscita di Emergenza" at the back of the facility.

The maintenance tunnels beneath Pompeii formed a modern labyrinth supporting the ancient city above. Service passages provided access to climate control systems, security infrastructure, and structural supports protecting the ruins. As they moved through the dimly lit corridors, Sam's mind raced through contingency plans.

"These tunnels connect most major excavation areas," Alessandra explained, leading them through a section reinforced with steel beams. "Maintenance staff use them to access infrastructure without disturbing tourists or archaeological sites."

Sam checked a facility map posted near a junction. "Where's the nearest exit?"

Alessandra pointed to a section labeled 'Area Servizi Orientale.' "The eastern service area. From there we can reach my vehicle."

As they navigated the passages, Danielle studied the structural supports with professional interest. "These reinforcement patterns are fascinating— they're maintaining tons of ancient stone above while minimizing impact on the archaeological integrity."

Even in crisis, her scientific mind remained engaged —one of the qualities Sam had always admired. Her ability to observe critical details under pressure had proven invaluable during their operations.

"The supporting architecture mirrors Roman engineering principles," Alessandra noted as they walked. "Modern solutions adapting ancient methods."

A distant metallic sound echoed through the tunnel, followed by voices—too far to distinguish words, but clearly suggesting pursuit.

"They've accessed the maintenance system," Sam whispered. "We need an alternative route."

Alessandra considered for a moment. "There's a secondary passage that leads to the Villa of the Mysteries excavation. It's further from my vehicle but less likely to be monitored."

They diverted at the next junction, taking a narrower passage sloping gradually upward. The temperature rose as they approached ground level, carrying the scent of sun-baked stone and Mediterranean vegetation.

"The Villa contains some of Pompeii's most significant frescoes," Alessandra explained softly as they moved. "Religious ceremonies, possibly initiation rites. Historically valuable, but also useful for our purposes—the site draws enough tourists to provide cover but not so many that movement is restricted."

They emerged through a service door disguised to match the surrounding stone, entering a quiet section of the ancient villa. Sam orientated himself quickly, noting two tour groups in adjacent rooms and calculating potential exit routes.

"This way," Alessandra directed, leading them toward what appeared to be a staff area. "My colleague Marcello should be working here today. He can provide transportation."

They moved through the villa, passing remarkable frescoes depicting mysterious ceremonies. Under different circumstances, Sam would have appreciated their artistic and historical significance. Now, he viewed everything through the lens of tactical advantage—crowds providing cover, narrow passages offering defensible positions, multiple exits ensuring escape options.

Alessandra's colleague Marcello, a bearded man in his early thirties wearing the uniform of the archaeological park staff, met them in a small office area. After a brief, hushed conversation in Italian, he nodded and led them toward a service vehicle parked behind the villa.

"He'll take us to my car at the secondary staff parking area," Alessandra explained. "Less obvious than the main visitor lot."

As they climbed into the maintenance vehicle, Sam's phone vibrated with an encrypted message. He checked it while Marcello navigated the service road that circled behind the main archaeological park.

"Our hotel reservation has been canceled," he told Danielle, translating the security alert. "Someone's accessed our information."

"We'll need alternative accommodation," Danielle said calmly, already considering options. She'd been through enough operations since 2011 to handle such setbacks with practiced efficiency, a far cry from those first traumatic days when she'd discovered Sam's true work during the East Coast Trek.

Alessandra leaned forward from the back seat. "I maintain a small apartment in Sorrento for research visits. It's registered under my mother's maiden name. You'll be secure there while planning your next moves."

Sam nodded gratefully. "We need to analyze what we've found and determine how it connects to the broader pattern of climate data manipulation."

As they left the archaeological park behind, Sam gazed back at Vesuvius looming over the landscape —a mountain that had buried truth once before, preserving it inadvertently for future discovery. The parallel wasn't lost on him. Sometimes, the most profound revelations remained hidden until the right moment, preserved beneath layers of deception until circumstances allowed their discovery.

The Consortium had been playing a generations-long game. Understanding its rules would require connecting patterns across centuries.

The terrace of Alessandra's Sorrento apartment offered a panoramic view of the Bay of Naples, with Vesuvius visible across the water. As evening descended, lights began twinkling along the coastline, creating a deceptively peaceful backdrop for their urgent work. The apartment itself was modest but comfortable, its walls lined with geological texts and volcanic research papers.

Danielle spread their collected documents across the dining table while Sam connected Alessandra's hard drive to his secure laptop. The volcanologist prepared espresso, the rich aroma filling the apartment as they organized their findings.

"If we overlay the manipulated climate data patterns from Copenhagen with what we've found in Italy, clear consistencies emerge," Sam noted, pulling up comparative charts on his screen. "The same methodological fingerprints appear across completely different historical periods."

Danielle examined thermal imaging scans from the museum archives. "The alteration techniques evolved over time, becoming more sophisticated as technology advanced. Early changes to historical records were relatively crude—changing numbers in published papers, selectively emphasizing certain studies over others."

"By the digital era, the manipulation became nearly undetectable," Alessandra added, placing espresso cups before them. "Document metadata retained no evidence of alteration. Only by comparing original physical records with digitized versions could inconsistencies be identified."

Sam sipped the strong coffee, organizing his thoughts. "The Consortium established a comprehensive system. First, alter historical baselines to create artificial context. Then, selectively manipulate current data collection points like the underwater monitors we found in Barbados."

"Creating a distorted picture that only they can see through," Danielle concluded. "Perfect information asymmetry."

Alessandra nodded. "While the world makes decisions based on manipulated data, the Consortium holds the accurate information— providing tremendous market advantage for resource allocation, agricultural investments, water rights..."

"And political leverage," Sam added. "Nations making binding commitments based on manipulated projections would be strategically vulnerable."

Thunder rumbled distantly over the bay as a summer storm approached, nature providing dramatic punctuation to their discussion. Danielle moved to close the terrace doors as rain began pattering against the tiles.

"We need to determine the authorization chain," she said, returning to the table. "Who approved these manipulations across so many different institutions and time periods?"

Sam pulled up the files extracted from the museum. "According to these access logs, changes to the Pompeii climate records required approval from a central academic committee based in Venice."

"Venice again," Danielle noted, sharing a meaningful look with Sam. "Marcus mentioned the 'Venice Sphere' containing master keys to the Consortium's operations."

Their shared history with Marcus stretched back to those first revelations in 2011, the beginning of their complicated journey as reluctant partners in Sam's world. How far they'd come since those painful early days, when trust had been shattered and slowly, painstakingly rebuilt.

"Venice has been a nexus of global trade information for centuries," Alessandra observed. "Historically, Venetian merchants maintained the most accurate maps and trade records in the Mediterranean, giving them significant advantages."

Sam's phone chimed with an encrypted message. He checked it, a slight smile forming. "Cade's algorithm has finished processing the numerical patterns in the altered records. He's identified a fractal encryption method linking the manipulations across multiple datasets."

He showed them the screen displaying a complex pattern of interlocking mathematical relationships. "These manipulations weren't random. They follow sophisticated mathematical patterns that maintain plausibility while serving specific objectives."

"It's beautiful, in a disturbing way," Danielle admitted, studying the elegant mathematical structure underlying the deception. "Like a Bach fugue composed of falsified data."

"Cade believes each pattern contains an authorization signature," Sam continued. "A mathematical fingerprint identifying who approved the manipulation."

The revelation shifted their understanding. This wasn't merely data alteration—it was a sophisticated system of encrypted authorizations spanning decades, hidden within the manipulations themselves.

Lightning flashed across the bay, momentarily illuminating Vesuvius in stark relief against the night sky. For centuries, the mountain had appeared dormant, concealing the volatile forces beneath. Sam couldn't help but see the parallel to their current situation—beneath the apparently stable systems of global climate research lay carefully hidden manipulations with the potential for devastating impact when finally exposed.

"We need to trace these authorization signatures to their source," he said, his determination hardening. "And Venice is clearly where they originate."

As the storm intensified outside, Sam watched Danielle working methodically through the evidence. After thirteen years of navigating this world together—first as reluctant co-parents maintaining operational security, then as partners slowly rebuilding trust—they had finally achieved the true partnership that once seemed impossible in those dark days of 2011. Looking at her now, fully committed to this mission that had become theirs, not just his, Sam felt a profound gratitude for their journey. The walls between his worlds had truly fallen, not just professionally but emotionally.

Morning brought clear skies and renewed purpose. After a secure video call with Cade, who provided enhanced analysis of the encryption patterns, they planned their next moves.

Alessandra had arranged a visit to a monitoring station on Vesuvius under her research authority, providing cover for examining current volcanic data collection methods.

The drive up Vesuvius offered spectacular views and strategic conversation opportunities. Alessandra's vehicle, a practical Alfa Romeo Stelvio in dark gray, navigated the winding road with confident precision as she explained the volcano's monitoring systems.

"The observatory maintains continuous measurements of ground temperature, gas emissions, and seismic activity," she explained. "This data feeds into global climate and geological databases."

"Making it another potential point for manipulation," Danielle observed.

"Precisely. After discovering historical discrepancies, I began comparing raw sensor readings with officially published data." Alessandra kept her eyes on the road as it curved around the mountain. "Subtle but systematic differences emerged—nothing dramatic enough to trigger alarms, but sufficient to influence long-term modeling."

They reached a security checkpoint where Alessandra presented her credentials. After a brief exchange with the guard, they were waved through to a modern facility built on the volcano's upper slopes.

The Vesuvius Observatory presented an unremarkable exterior—a utilitarian structure housing sophisticated monitoring equipment. Inside, technicians monitored computer displays showing real-time data from sensors distributed across the volcano. Alessandra introduced Sam and Danielle as visiting Canadian researchers assisting her comparative study.

"Dr. Moretti is in the main monitoring room," a young technician informed Alessandra. "He's expecting you."

Dr. Gabriele Moretti, the observatory's assistant director, greeted them with professional courtesy. In his fifties, with prematurely gray hair and the intense focus common to dedicated scientists, he showed them to a conference room overlooking the crater.

"Your research proposal is quite interesting," he said, reviewing Alessandra's paperwork. "Comparing seismic influences on atmospheric gas measurements across different volcanic systems has potential applications for climate modeling."

"That's precisely our interest," Alessandra confirmed smoothly. "Particularly how these measurements interface with broader climate databases."

Moretti nodded. "I've provided access to our primary systems. You'll have read-only privileges for today's visit."

After he left, Alessandra guided them to a workstation in the corner of the main monitoring room. "This terminal can access the raw sensor data before it enters the publication pipeline."

Sam and Danielle positioned themselves to shield the screen from casual observation while Alessandra navigated the system. Her fingers moved efficiently through database queries, extracting temperature and gas composition measurements from the past five years.

"Here," she said quietly, indicating a section of data. "Notice the pattern in the carbon dioxide measurements."

Danielle studied the numbers, her scientific training immediately spotting the anomaly. "The official publications show less variability than the raw readings."

"Smoothing the peaks and valleys," Sam observed. "Making the patterns appear more stable than they actually are."

"This manipulation serves two purposes—it makes natural variations appear less significant, which in turn makes anthropogenic changes seem more anomalous."

Alessandra nodded, continuing to navigate through the system, extracting data to a secure drive disguised as standard research collection. As she worked, Sam noticed Dr. Moretti watching them from across the room, his attention seemingly casual but persistent.

"We have company," Sam murmured. "Eleven o'clock, gray sweater."

Danielle nodded imperceptibly. "I noticed. He's made three passes by this station in ten minutes." Years of operational awareness had honed her ability to track potential threats while appearing absorbed in other tasks—a skill she'd been developing since those first difficult days of adjusting to Sam's world in 2011.

Alessandra continued working, her expression revealing nothing. "Almost finished. I'm accessing the authorization protocols now."

Her screen displayed a security gateway requiring additional credentials. She entered a complex password, gaining access to a restricted area of the system.

"There," she said softly. "The authorization chain for data publication."

The screen displayed a hierarchical structure showing approval pathways for data moving from raw collection to public databases. At the top of the chain sat an innocuous label: "VCRC Final Authorization."

"VCRC?" Danielle questioned.

"Venice Climate Research Consortium," Alessandra explained. "Officially, an international oversight body ensuring data consistency across research institutions."

"And unofficially?" Sam asked.

"The perfect mechanism for centralized control of climate information."

Dr. Moretti approached their workstation, a polite smile masking evident concern. "Finding everything you need, Professor Bianchi?"

"Yes, thank you," Alessandra replied smoothly. "The correlation between seismic activity and gas emissions is quite revealing."

"Indeed." Moretti's gaze lingered on their screen, which Alessandra had quickly switched to a standard data visualization. "I'm particularly interested in your comparative methodology. Perhaps you could explain it over lunch? Our cafeteria has a rather impressive view of Naples."

The invitation was clearly meant to separate them from the computer. Alessandra smiled professionally. "That would be lovely. We've just about finished our initial data collection."

As they followed Moretti toward the cafeteria, Sam caught Danielle's eye. The slight nod confirmed she'd reached the same conclusion—their interest had been noticed, and their time at the observatory would be limited.

The facility cafeteria featured floor-to-ceiling windows overlooking the Bay of Naples, offering a panoramic vista that would normally command appreciation. Today, Sam assessed it primarily for tactical considerations—limited exit options, numerous witnesses, and the long, winding road that provided the only vehicle access to the facility.

Over a lunch of pasta and local wine, Moretti engaged them in seemingly casual conversation about Canadian research institutions and climate science priorities. His questions, while professionally appropriate, contained subtle probes about their backgrounds and specific interests.

"Your focus on historical data comparison is intriguing," he noted. "Not many researchers examine the relationship between volcanic records and broader climate patterns."

"Historical baselines provide essential context for current observations," Danielle replied, matching his professional tone. "Accuracy in those baselines determines the validity of all subsequent modeling."

Something flickered in Moretti's eyes—recognition, perhaps, of the implication behind her statement. He smiled thinly. "Accuracy, of course, must be balanced with methodology consistency. Raw data often requires calibration to account for collection variables."

"Calibration or correction?" Alessandra asked innocently, though Sam caught the deliberate challenge in her question.

Moretti's smile remained fixed. "A matter of scientific perspective, I suppose."

The conversation maintained its veneer of collegiality, but the undercurrents were unmistakable. By the time they finished lunch, Sam had counted three text notifications on Moretti's phone, each prompting subtle changes in his demeanor.

"I hope you've gathered sufficient data for your initial research," Moretti said as they prepared to leave. "Unfortunately, we have a system update scheduled for this afternoon that will take our databases offline."

The abrupt termination of their access confirmed Sam's suspicions. They were being politely expelled before they could dig deeper.

"We've collected enough for our preliminary analysis," Alessandra assured him. "Thank you for your hospitality."

As they drove down the winding road from the observatory, Sam noticed a vehicle pulling out behind them.

"We're being followed," he noted calmly. "Black SUV, two occupants."

Alessandra checked her mirror. "Standard security protocol or something more concerning?"

"Let's find out." Sam studied the road ahead. "When you reach the next switchback, accelerate through the turn instead of braking. If they match your unusual driving pattern..."

Alessandra nodded, understanding the surveillance detection technique. As they approached the sharp curve, she maintained speed longer than normal driving would dictate, then accelerated through the turn—a counter-intuitive move that would be mimicked only by someone focused on following rather than coincidentally taking the same route.

The black SUV matched their pattern precisely.

"Definitely following," Danielle confirmed, watching through the side mirror. "Professional technique, too. They're maintaining optimal surveillance distance."

Alessandra remained calm, her hands steady on the wheel. "Options?"

Sam considered their position. "We need to reach Pompeii before they can intercept us. From there, we can use the tourist crowds for cover."

"And if they try to stop us before we reach Pompeii?"

"Then we discover whether this vehicle has the handling capabilities claimed in the brochure," Sam replied with grim humor.

Alessandra's slight smile suggested confidence in both her vehicle and her driving skills. "Italian engineering against Italian roads—a fair contest."

She increased their speed, navigating the curves with precision that revealed considerable experience with the mountain roads. The SUV matched their pace, neither gaining nor losing ground— professional surveillance maintaining optimal position.

"They're not trying to intercept," Sam observed. "Just track our movements."

"Waiting for a better opportunity," Danielle suggested. "Or reinforcements."

As they approached the base of the mountain, Alessandra made an unexpected decision. Instead of continuing toward Pompeii, she turned onto a smaller local road.

"Shortcut?" Sam asked.

"Alternative destination," she replied. "If they're tracking us to identify safe locations, we shouldn't lead them to either Pompeii or my apartment."

The narrow road wound through olive groves and small villages, eventually emerging near the coast south of Pompeii. The SUV maintained its pursuit, though at a greater distance on the narrower roads.

"Where are we headed?" Danielle asked.

"Herculaneum," Alessandra answered. "Like Pompeii, buried by Vesuvius, but preserved differently—mudflows rather than ash. The site contains distinct climate records that might provide additional validation."

"And significant tourist presence for cover," Sam noted with approval.

"Precisely."

The road curved around the coastline, offering breathtaking views that belied their tense situation. Eventually, they reached the modern town of Ercolano, built directly above the ancient ruins of Herculaneum.

Alessandra navigated through narrow streets to a public parking area near the archaeological site. "We'll approach on foot. The excavation is smaller than Pompeii but equally significant—and contains research facilities with climate record access."

As they exited the vehicle, Sam scanned for the SUV. It had maintained distance but remained visible, parking at the far end of the lot.

"Two men, business casual attire, moving to intercept on foot," he reported quietly. "We need to reach the site entrance before they close distance."

They moved at a brisk tourist pace toward the ticket area, merging with a German tour group purchasing entrance passes. Alessandra spoke briefly with the ticket attendant, showing her research credentials, and they were waved through a staff entrance while the followers were still navigating the main ticket line.

"My research access extends to all Vesuvian archaeological sites," Alessandra explained as they entered the ancient city. "We have perhaps fifteen minutes before they follow through the main entrance."

Herculaneum presented a different aspect than Pompeii—smaller but better preserved, with multi-story buildings and carbonized wooden features that had survived the catastrophic burial. Alessandra led them efficiently through the site toward a modern structure built unobtrusively at the periphery.

"The conservation laboratory," she explained. "It houses climate-controlled storage for organic materials recovered from the site—wooden objects, fabrics, papyri—along with environmental records documenting preservation conditions."

She used her credentials to access the facility, leading them through a reception area where she exchanged brief greetings with staff before proceeding to a research room equipped with computers and specialized scanning equipment.

"Herculaneum's preservation offers unique climate insights," she explained as she accessed the system. "The mudflows preserved organic materials that provide direct evidence of environmental conditions before the eruption."

"Different preservation method, same data manipulation?" Danielle asked.

"Let's find out."

Alessandra navigated through the database, accessing records of seed samples, pollen analyses, and tree ring studies from preserved wooden beams. She compared these with published climate reconstructions based on the same evidence.

"The pattern continues," she confirmed after several minutes. "The raw data shows greater climate variability than the published reconstructions. The same mathematical smoothing appears in the differential."

Sam examined the authorization chain displayed in the corner of one report. "And the final approval comes from..."

"The Venice Climate Research Consortium," Alessandra confirmed. "Every significant climate record from the Mediterranean region passes through their authorization protocol."

Danielle studied the mathematical adjustments applied to the raw data. "These manipulations follow the same fractal pattern Cade identified—subtle enough to appear as legitimate calibration to most researchers, but systematically shifting baseline assumptions."

"With cascading effects on all subsequent climate modeling," Sam added. "Brilliant and terrifying in its comprehensiveness."

A notification appeared on Alessandra's phone. She checked it, her expression tightening. "Security alert. Someone just accessed the site using administrator credentials that should be inactive. Our followers have technological support."

Sam immediately began gathering their evidence while Danielle photographed key documents displayed on the screen. "How many exits?"

"Main entrance and staff access at the rear," Alessandra replied, downloading critical files to a secure drive. "The rear exits to a maintenance area near the modern town."

They finished collecting evidence and moved toward the rear exit, passing through a laboratory where conservators were carefully cleaning artifacts. No one questioned their presence as Alessandra's credentials provided legitimate access.

The rear door opened to a small parking area where maintenance vehicles were stored. Beyond lay the streets of modern Ercolano, offering countless routes for evasion.

"We should separate temporarily," Sam suggested. "Danielle and I will take public transportation to Naples. Can you secure alternative transportation?"

Alessandra nodded. "I have colleagues in Naples who can assist. We'll rendezvous at the secondary location we discussed."

They agreed on communication protocols and parted ways, Sam and Danielle heading toward the Circumvesuviana train station while Alessandra took a different route through the town. As they walked briskly through the narrow streets, Sam reflected on how the past and present intertwined in their investigation—ancient volcanic destruction preserving evidence that might now help prevent a modern catastrophe.

The train to Naples offered a brief respite and planning opportunity. In the rattling carriage carrying tourists and commuters, Sam and Danielle sat close together, speaking softly beneath the ambient noise.

"The pattern is consistent across every dataset we've examined," Danielle noted. "Historical records manipulated to minimize natural variations, creating artificial baselines against which current changes can be exaggerated or minimized depending on the Consortium's objectives."

Sam nodded. "And always with final authorization from Venice. Marcus was right—whatever controls the entire system is there."

"The Venice Sphere," Danielle murmured.

Outside the train window, Vesuvius loomed against the blue sky—a constant reminder of nature's power to preserve truth as well as destroy it. In the shadow of the mountain that had buried Pompeii and Herculaneum, they had uncovered evidence of manipulation spanning centuries—layers of deception that, like the volcanic ash itself, had inadvertently preserved the very truth it sought to conceal.

Their next destination was clear. Venice—where the threads of manipulation converged, where Marcus had directed them, and where the answers to generations of deception awaited discovery.

As the train carried them toward Naples, Sam's thoughts turned to their children—to Ellie's environmental passion, Rae's linguistic insights, Cade's algorithmic brilliance, and Mackie's spatial perception. Each possessed talents that, unknowingly, had prepared them for this very struggle. The patterns Carmichael had recognized in Sam's generation had evolved in the next, creating capabilities uniquely suited to unraveling the Consortium's web.

"You're thinking about the kids," Danielle said, recognizing his expression—a familiarity born of their long, complicated journey together.

Sam nodded. "How everything they are—everything we've nurtured in them—seems destined for this moment."

"Not destined," Danielle corrected, resting her hand on his arm—a gesture that would have been unthinkable during those first painful years after 2011. "Prepared. There's a difference."

Her distinction was important. Destiny suggested lack of choice—the very manipulation they were fighting against. Preparation offered readiness while preserving freedom of action. They'd learned this lesson painfully over thirteen years, from the traumatic discovery in 2011 to their gradual rebuilding of trust.

As Naples came into view, Sam settled on their next move. They would rendezvous with Alessandra, analyze their combined findings, and prepare for Venice—where the heart of the Consortium's climate manipulation would finally be exposed.

The shadow of Vesuvius receded behind them, but its lessons remained. Sometimes truth lay buried, waiting for those prepared to recognize its patterns when finally revealed. Just as their marriage had weathered its eruption thirteen years ago and emerged stronger, transformed by the pressure and heat of crisis into something more resilient than before.

Chapter 8
The Cipher Collapses
July-August 2024

Dawn stretched golden fingers across Rome's ancient skyline as Sam Clayton leaned against the weathered stone balustrade of their hotel room. Sleep had eluded him, his mind churning through the revelations from Naples and Pompeii. The morning air carried the scent of fresh bread and coffee from the café below, mingling with the distinctive aroma of a city that had witnessed millennia of secrets.

Danielle emerged onto the balcony, her chestnut curls caught in the morning light. She offered a steaming espresso, the ceramic warm against his palm.

"You've been up for hours," she said, not a question but an observation.

Sam nodded, accepting both the coffee and the unspoken understanding that had grown between them since Italy. The woman who stood beside him now was neither the unsuspecting spouse of Copenhagen nor the reluctant partner of their fractured post-2011 years. She had become something else entirely—his operational equal, a transformation that had been years in the making but had fully crystallized in these weeks in Rome.

"Cade's algorithm detected something last night," Sam said, keeping his voice low despite the privacy of their balcony. "Data bursts from the Consortium's networks that match patterns we saw in Pompeii."

Danielle's gaze sharpened. "They're moving the Venice Sphere?"

"Or realizing we're closing in on it." Sam sipped the bitter espresso, letting it fortify him. "Cade sent an update at three this morning. He's been analyzing the fractals from the authorization signatures we found at Vesuvius. There's a pattern that repeats across all of them—too consistent to be coincidence, too complex to be standard procedure."

"And exactly the kind of elegance that would appeal to someone like Roshkov," Danielle added, her scientific mind connecting the pieces.

Below them, Rome was awakening—delivery trucks navigating narrow streets, shopkeepers raising shutters, tourists already gathering with maps and cameras. The ancient city had seen empires rise and fall, kept secrets for centuries. Now it would serve as their final operational base before Venice.

Sam's phone vibrated with a message from an unknown number: American Embassy. Cultural Affairs Office. 10:00 hours. Bring the Naples files.

The dance had begun.

The American Embassy in Rome occupied a Renaissance-era building appropriately positioned between the ancient Forum and the modern EUR district—a bridge between worlds, much like their operation itself. Sam and Danielle approached separately, tourists among tourists, with practiced nonchalance that concealed hypervigilance.

The Cultural Affairs Office proved to be a wood-paneled room with diplomatic photographs covering strategic surveillance points. A short, balding man with wire-rimmed glasses introduced himself only as Phillips.

"Professor Clayton," he said, shaking Sam's hand firmly. The grip communicated more than the words —a subtle pressure pattern that confirmed his authorization level. "And Mrs. Clayton. Your research on Renaissance painting techniques has generated considerable interest."

The cover established, they followed Phillips through a hidden door behind a bookcase, down a narrow corridor, and into a soundproofed room with modern communication equipment disguised as ordinary office technology.

"Secure for thirty minutes," Phillips said, his voice shifting from diplomatic pleasantry to operational precision. "After that, standard exit protocols apply."

Sam connected the drive containing their Naples findings to the specialized terminal. "We need verification and distribution."

Phillips nodded. "Your son's algorithm has already been validated by our technical team. Remarkable work for someone his age."

"He doesn't know the full scope," Danielle said, protective instinct evident in her voice despite her years of operational awareness. "He thinks he's helping with environmental research."

"For now," Sam added quietly, exchanging a glance with Danielle that acknowledged their evolving approach to family involvement.

The screen illuminated with Cade's fractals—mathematical patterns that revealed the subtle manipulations in climate data across decades. Each dataset manipulation carried its unique signature, yet all contained an elegantly embedded authorization code visible only when viewed through Cade's specialized algorithm.

"The Consortium has been manipulating climate data systematically since the 1950s," Sam explained. "But they've evolved from crude alterations to sophisticated mathematical distortions that maintain plausibility while serving specific objectives."

"Perfect information asymmetry," Phillips said, examining the patterns. "They see the real data while everyone else acts on manipulated predictions."

"Exactly what Cade said," Danielle noted with pride tinged with concern.

Phillips tapped commands into the terminal, establishing secure connections to intelligence agencies across three continents. "The authentication protocols are active. We have fourteen minutes to complete primary distribution."

"The Naples archaeological evidence confirms historical manipulation creating false baselines," Sam continued. "Pompeii's preserved records provide unaltered climate information from Roman times. When compared with official databases, the pattern of falsification becomes unmistakable."

"And these manipulations always serve the same purpose," Danielle added with the confidence of someone who had spent over a decade gradually piecing together the operational puzzle. "Creating artificial resource scarcities in specific regions where Consortium members have strategic interests."

Phillips's eyes narrowed behind his glasses. "The question is why 'K' would authorize exposure after all this time. The Consortium's structure has always protected its leadership through compartmentalization."

"Kessler isn't just protecting the Consortium," Sam said. "Based on the authorization pathways we've tracked, he's systematically eliminating older operational controllers—people who know too much."

"Including your father," Phillips said.

Sam's jaw tightened. "Carmichael became a liability when he discovered the full scope of the Venice Sphere."

Phillips distributed the final data packets and initiated the terminal's security wipe. "Seven minutes remaining. There's something else you should see."

He retrieved a secure tablet from a hidden compartment. "This arrived yesterday through channels we thought were compromised since Brussels."

The video displayed a timestamp from six weeks ago. The face that appeared on the screen sent an electric shock through Sam's system—Marcus Cartier, his mentor, supposedly dead since 2022.

"Hello, Sam." Marcus's voice carried the same quiet authority Sam remembered from their first meeting at the print shop decades earlier. "If you're seeing this, you've followed the breadcrumbs exactly as anticipated. The music truly does continue between the notes."

Sam felt Danielle's hand slip into his, anchoring him as Marcus continued. Her gesture contained thirteen years of shared understanding about this world she had once violently rejected but gradually accepted as part of their shared reality.

"The Consortium's climate manipulation was never the ultimate objective, merely their methodology. The true purpose has always been control of critical resources—water, agriculture, energy—through market manipulation based on falsified projections. Kessler elevated this from profitable exploitation to global resource domination."

Marcus's face showed subtle signs of aging since Sam had last seen him, but his eyes remained intensely focused. "Your recruitment wasn't coincidence, Sam. Your childhood aptitude tests showed remarkable pattern recognition and analytical capabilities. Carmichael recognized these traits—he'd seen them in himself. When you took that summer job at my print shop during your Clarkson years, it wasn't chance that brought you there."

Sam felt the foundations of his personal history shifting beneath him. The random events that had shaped his life—the summer job, meeting Danielle, his teaching career—suddenly revealed as carefully orchestrated steps in a larger design.

"Your children have developed exactly as we hoped," Marcus continued. "The genetic inheritance patterns were always theoretical until your family confirmed them. Ellie's environmental analysis, Rae's linguistic capabilities, Cade's algorithmic thinking, young Mackie's spatial awareness—each representing specialized neural development we've tracked across three generations."

"They've been watching us our entire lives," Danielle whispered, her scientific mind grasping the implications instantly, her voice containing the same intensity it had that night in 2011 when she'd first discovered Sam's double life.

"Not watching," Sam corrected, the pieces falling into place with terrible clarity. "Cultivating."

Marcus's recorded image leaned forward. "The Venice Sphere contains everything—the complete operational structure, financial trails, falsified datasets, and most critically, the master encryption keys that would expose every Consortium agent globally. Kessler knows you're coming for it, Sam. He's anticipated everything—except perhaps the variable represented by your family's involvement."

The video abruptly ended, leaving behind coordinates embedded in the final frame. Phillips immediately transferred them to an encrypted drive.

"Time's up," he said, initiating final security protocols. "Standard exit procedures. Your next contact will be at the Palazzo Barberini tomorrow at 15:00 hours. Art history tour, north wing."

The Villa Borghese Gardens provided both strategic surveillance advantage and the perfect cover for necessary conversation. Sam and Danielle walked the gravel paths as afternoon sun filtered through ancient pines, creating shifting patterns of light and shadow that mirrored Sam's turbulent thoughts.

"You're wondering if any of it was real," Danielle said, reading his silence with the intuition of someone who had navigated the complexities of their relationship for thirteen years since the traumatic discovery in 2011. "Our meeting, our marriage, our children."

Sam watched a family nearby—tourists with an energetic toddler chasing pigeons. "Thirty years together, and I never questioned how we met. That holiday party at SUNY Plattsburgh—was that orchestrated too?"

"Does it matter?" Danielle stopped, turning to face him directly. "Whatever brought us together, what we built is ours. The family we created, the life we shared—those are real, Sam."

Her certainty steadied him, reminding him of how far they'd come from those terrible days in 2011 when their marriage had nearly collapsed under the weight of his secrets. "How are you not angry about this? Your mother's involvement, your family's intelligence connections—all kept from you until 2011."

"Oh, I'm furious," Danielle said, a flash of genuine emotion breaking through her operational composure. "But right now, that's a luxury we can't afford. I'll have my reckoning with my mother when this is finished."

Sam nodded, recognizing the steel beneath her calm exterior—the same quality that had made her such a formidable partner in this operation, despite the years they'd spent emotionally distant while co-parenting their children.

"Marcus said they were cultivating genetic traits across generations," he said, lowering his voice as they continued walking. "Carmichael's musical abilities evolving into my programming skills, then appearing as specialized talents in our children."

"That's not how genetics works," Danielle countered, her scientific background asserting itself. "Environmental factors, education, nurture versus nature—it's infinitely more complex than simple inheritance patterns."

"Unless they know something we don't," Sam said. "The Consortium has been manipulating information for decades. What if their understanding of genetic inheritance patterns is similarly advanced?"

Danielle considered this, her analytical mind visibly processing the implications. "Either way, our children aren't experiments or assets. They're people making their own choices."

"Which is exactly what makes them unpredictable to Kessler," Sam realized. "The Consortium thrives on controlling variables, predicting outcomes. Our family represents too many unknown factors."

They reached a secluded viewpoint overlooking the Spanish Steps, the city spread before them in geometric patterns that seemed suddenly meaningful—streets and buildings forming interconnected systems much like the data structures they'd been unraveling.

"Venice is next," Sam said, the pieces of their operation falling into place. "The Sphere will be heavily protected, possibly moved already based on Cade's detection of network activity."

"If Kessler knows we're coming, walking into Venice feels like walking into a trap," Danielle observed with the tactical assessment of someone who had gradually developed operational perspective since 2011.

"Which is exactly why we need to arrive from an unexpected direction." Sam pulled out his phone, sending a message to the secure account Cade had established: Begin Moonlight Sonata protocol. Coordinate with R to confirm location. Operational window: 72 hours.

The Palazzo Barberini's north wing housed a collection of Renaissance masterpieces that provided both cultural enrichment and operational cover. Sam and Danielle joined an English-language tour group, maintaining the appearance of academic interest while conducting surveillance sweeps of the ornate galleries.

Their guide, a petite woman with steel-gray hair and penetrating blue eyes, approached as they studied a Caravaggio.

"The chiaroscuro technique reveals details hidden in darkness," she said in flawless British English. "Notice how light illuminates only what the artist wishes you to see."

The recognition phrase delivered, Sam responded with the appropriate counter. "While the observer must imagine what remains in shadow."

"Indeed, Professor Clayton." She handed them a gallery brochure with a handwritten notation about a special exhibition. "The Murano glass display is particularly impressive. Sixteenth-century Venetian techniques created pieces of remarkable clarity."

Sam nodded, understanding the oblique confirmation of the Venice Sphere's location. The guide moved on to the next painting, her role completed in the exchange that had taken less than thirty seconds.

As they followed the tour through arched doorways into the next gallery, Sam's phone vibrated with an incoming message—a series of code fragments from Cade that translated to: Patterns confirmed. Data pathway identified. Venice server accessed. Awaiting final coordinates.

The message confirmed that Cade had successfully penetrated the Consortium's outer security ring—a remarkable achievement that filled Sam with both pride and apprehension. Every boundary they crossed brought their children closer to the dangerous world Sam had tried to shield them from, even as Danielle had gradually argued for greater transparency over the years.

"He figured it out," Sam whispered to Danielle. "Using those fractals from Naples as access points."

"Of course he did," Danielle replied with quiet confidence. "He's your son." The subtle emphasis contained layers of meaning—acknowledgment of genetic inheritance alongside recognition of how far they'd come in their journey as a family.

The tour concluded in a small, circular room with a magnificent painted ceiling depicting The Triumph of Divine Providence—gods and mortals interconnected in a cosmic dance of fate and free will. Sam found the symbolism uncomfortably apt.

As the group dispersed, a museum guard approached with practiced indifference. "Professor

Clayton, your private viewing of the conservation laboratory has been arranged. This way, please."

They followed him through a staff door, down a service corridor, and into a windowless room dominated by sophisticated imaging equipment. A dark-haired man in a technician's coat stood examining high-resolution scans of artwork.

"The Vatican analysis confirms your findings," he said without preamble, his accent marking him as Italian intelligence. "The pattern of document alteration extends throughout their historical climate archives—subtle changes that would be undetectable without your son's algorithm."

He displayed a series of images showing temperature and rainfall records from the 1800s, the manipulations visible only when highlighted by Cade's fractal pattern detection.

"All manipulated records show final authorization from the Venice Climate Research Consortium," the technician continued, bringing up the organizational chart they'd been assembling piece by piece since Naples. "That confirms Venice as the central control point, just as your intelligence suggested."

"And the facility location?" Sam asked.

"Murano Island. A functioning glass factory provides cover for an underground data center." The technician displayed architectural schematics that reminded Sam painfully of Mackie's detailed drawings. "The Venice Sphere itself is likely stored in this secure vault beneath the main furnace room."

"Thermal masking," Danielle noted with the assurance of someone who had been gradually integrating scientific expertise with operational knowledge for over a decade. "The heat from the glass production would hide any signature from the server farm."

"Exactly." The technician handed Sam a specialized data drive. "This contains building schematics, security patrol patterns, and access codes for peripheral systems. The primary authorization keys will require direct extraction."

Sam pocketed the drive. "Our window is closing. Kessler will move the Sphere if he detects our approach."

"Which is why you won't be approaching at all," came a voice from the doorway.

Sam turned, his body automatically shifting to protective stance before his mind registered the speaker—Ivan Roshkov, elegant as always in a tailored gray suit, his pale eyes evaluating them with clinical precision.

"Fascinating to finally meet the wife behind the operative," Roshkov said, nodding to Danielle. "Your involvement has added an unpredictable variable to this equation, Mrs. Clayton."

"That's Dr. Clayton, actually," Danielle corrected, her calm belying the tension Sam could feel radiating from her. "And I find unpredictability has its advantages in certain scenarios."

A ghost of a smile crossed Roshkov's face. "Indeed. Much like quantum mechanics—the observer affects the system merely by observing."

Sam maintained his position between Roshkov and Danielle. "Last I checked, you were Kessler's Director of Strategic Resources. Interesting company you're keeping these days."

"Appearances, Mr. Clayton. Something you understand quite well." Roshkov moved further into the room, each step precisely calculated. "I've been inside Kessler's organization since Copenhagen, playing a much deeper game than either side realized."

"Why reveal yourself now?" Sam asked, not relaxing his guard.

"Because in approximately forty-eight hours, Kessler will transfer the Venice Sphere to a new location—one even I am not privy to." Roshkov withdrew a small device from his pocket, placing it carefully on the examination table. "This will provide access to the Murano facility's main security grid for exactly seven minutes tomorrow night, during the annual Masquerade Ball at La Fenice."

Sam didn't reach for the device. "Why would you help us?"

"I'm not helping you, Mr. Clayton. I'm securing my own interests." Roshkov straightened his already immaculate cuffs. "Kessler's resource manipulation strategies have evolved from market advantage to something far more destructive. The elimination of your father was merely the beginning of a systematic purge of anyone with knowledge of the original climate data operation."

"You're on the list," Danielle deduced.

"As is everyone connected to the early phases," Roshkov confirmed. "Your Marcus Cartier recognized this pattern years ago. His 'death' in

Brussels was a necessary precaution, as was your father's contingency planning."

The pieces aligned in Sam's mind with terrible clarity. "Carmichael knew this before his memory began to fade. All those saxophones, the hidden messages—he was preparing for this moment for years."

"Generations," Roshkov corrected. "Your recruitment wasn't Marcus's initiative, Mr. Clayton. It was your father's design from the beginning."

The room seemed to tilt beneath Sam's feet as decades of his life rearranged themselves into a pattern he hadn't recognized until now.

"The masquerade at La Fenice provides optimal cover," Roshkov continued, professional despite the bombshell he'd delivered. "Traditional Venetian masks, hundreds of guests, minimized facial recognition capability. The security grid will open at precisely 21:17, coordinated with the evening's fireworks display over the Grand Canal."

"And your role in all this?" Sam asked, still processing.

"Plausible deniability. I'll be visibly elsewhere, ensuring my continued value to whatever remains of the Consortium after your operation concludes." Roshkov moved toward the door. "One final piece of information you should consider: Richard Kessler is not the ultimate authority within the Consortium. He answers to a council whose identities are contained within the Venice Sphere."

"Why tell us this?" Danielle asked.

"Because chess is only interesting when both players have sufficient information to make meaningful choices." Roshkov paused at the threshold. "Do svidaniya, Mr. and Mrs. Clayton. I suspect our paths will cross again under different circumstances."

After he departed, silence hung in the room as Sam and Danielle exchanged glances that contained volumes of unspoken understanding built through thirteen years of navigating their complex relationship.

"Can we trust him?" Danielle finally asked.

"Absolutely not," Sam replied. "But his information has proven accurate before."

"So we use it, but plan for betrayal," she concluded with the pragmatism that had gradually replaced her initial shock and anger from 2011.

Sam nodded, his mind already mapping contingencies. "We'll need to contact Cade again—his algorithm can verify the security protocols on this device before we implement anything."

"And then Venice," Danielle said. "The Masquerade Ball at La Fenice."

"Where everyone wears a mask," Sam agreed, "while playing roles they've rehearsed their entire lives."

Night had fallen by the time they returned to their hotel, Rome's ancient streets illuminated by a blend of historic lanterns and modern lighting that created pools of brightness amid comfortable shadow. The day's revelations had left Sam with a restlessness that no amount of operational planning could dispel.

In their room, Danielle secured the standard privacy protocols while Sam established the secure channel to contact Cade. Their son's face appeared on the encrypted laptop screen, his blonde curls disheveled in the way that always happened when he was deep in a coding project. Despite the serious circumstances, Sam felt a surge of affection at the familiar sight.

"Dad, Mom," Cade greeted them, his expression indicating he'd been waiting for their call. "The fractals from Naples unlocked something bigger than we thought. The climate data manipulation isn't just alteration—it's selective redirection."

"Meaning what exactly?" Danielle asked, leaning closer to the screen.

"They're operating a dual-channel system," Cade explained, his hands moving as he talked in the animated way they did when he was explaining complex concepts. "The public-facing data shows manipulated climate projections, but the Consortium maintains access to the actual readings. It creates —"

"Perfect information asymmetry," Sam finished, remembering Phillips's words from earlier. "They know the actual environmental conditions while everyone else acts on false projections."

"Exactly," Cade confirmed, eyes bright with the puzzle-solver's satisfaction. "And I found something else—a pattern within the authorization signatures themselves. It's like a fractal encryption system where each level of authorization contains the key to the next level, but only if you know exactly where to look."

Cade displayed a series of mathematical models that spiraled in elegant complexity—the same patterns they'd discovered in Naples, now expanded into a multidimensional framework that revealed the Consortium's hierarchical authorization structure.

"Roshkov was telling the truth," Danielle murmured. "Kessler isn't at the top."

"There's a council above him," Sam agreed. "And the Venice Sphere contains their identities."

"Speaking of which," Cade continued, "that security device you sent—it's legitimate, but it's also incomplete. It'll provide access to the main security grid, but there's a secondary system that operates independently. You'll need this modified access protocol to bypass both."

He transmitted a code sequence that appeared on their secure drive. Sam recognized his son's programming style—elegant, efficient, with subtle creative flourishes that reminded him of Carmichael's jazz improvisations.

"How did you figure this out?" Sam asked, professional admiration mixing with parental pride.

Cade shrugged with the casual confidence of youth. "The Consortium's encryption is sophisticated, but it follows predictable patterns once you identify the underlying mathematical structure. It's beautiful in its way—like Bach composing with data."

The same phrase Danielle had used in Pompeii, Sam noted—another example of inherited patterns of thought that seemed increasingly significant.

"Cade," Danielle said carefully, "how much do you understand about what we're really doing here?"

Their son's expression grew more serious, the boyishness temporarily replaced by something older and more knowing. "More than you've told me. The climate data manipulation, the Consortium's resource control operations, Grandpa's involvement —I've been connecting dots for a while now."

Sam felt a complex mixture of regret and relief. "We were trying to protect you."

"I know," Cade said simply. "But maybe it's time to consider that we're stronger together than separated by secrets."

The wisdom in his words—so adult, so perceptive— hit Sam with unexpected force. The compartmentalization he'd maintained for decades was crumbling from multiple directions, revealing that the walls he'd built to protect his family had perhaps been unnecessary all along.

"We'll talk about everything when we get home," Sam promised. "All of it."

Cade nodded, then glanced off-screen as if checking something. "The security window for this connection is closing. One more thing—I've set up a background process that will monitor the Murano facility's power consumption. If they start transferring data from the main servers, we'll know immediately."

"Smart thinking," Danielle said with obvious pride.

"Stay safe," Cade said, suddenly looking like the child Sam still saw him as, despite his growing capabilities. "Both of you."

The connection ended, leaving Sam and Danielle in momentary silence.

"He's been figuring it out all along," Sam finally said.

"They all have, in their ways," Danielle replied. "We've been so focused on protecting them that we missed how capable they've become."

Sam moved to the balcony, looking out over the eternal city with its layers of history visible in stone and light. The ancient Romans had understood the concept of legacy—building for future generations, creating structures that would outlast their creators. Carmichael, it seemed, had operated with similar foresight.

"Venice tomorrow," he said as Danielle joined him. "The final piece of Carmichael's puzzle."

"And then what?" she asked. "When this is over—if we succeed—what happens to us? To our family?"

The question caught Sam unprepared, focused as he'd been on the operation itself rather than its aftermath. The future beyond the Venice Sphere had remained deliberately unexamined.

"I don't know," he admitted. "For thirty years, I've lived divided between my teaching and this other world. But maybe Cade's right—maybe the strength is in integration, not separation."

Danielle leaned against him, her presence solid and reassuring. "Whatever comes next, we face it together. No more separate worlds."

The phrase held deeper meaning now—not just about information sharing, but about the emotional reconciliation they had been gradually working toward since the traumatic discovery in 2011. This mission to Venice represented not just the culmination of an operational journey, but the final healing of their long-fractured relationship.

Below them, Rome continued its eternal rhythms—a city that had witnessed empires rise and fall, secrets buried and unearthed. Tomorrow they would travel to Venice for the culmination of an operation decades in the making. But tonight, they stood together on a balcony above the ancient streets, two people finding strength in connection rather than division.

For the first time since Carmichael's mind had slipped away, Sam felt a sense of clarity about the path ahead—not because he could see where it led, but because he no longer walked it alone.

Chapter 9
Venetian Masquerade
August 2024

Morning light shimmered across the Grand Canal as Sam leaned against the weathered stone balcony of their corner suite. Behind him, Danielle methodically arranged their formal attire for tonight's masquerade ball, each movement precise and purposeful. The rising sun painted Venice's timeworn facades in shades of amber and gold, the ancient city awakening to another day of secrets hidden beneath magnificent beauty.

"It's perfect," Sam said, his eyes tracking a vintage Riva Aquariva gliding beneath the Bridge of the Barefoot Monks. "Centuries of intrigue embedded in every stone. A city built on masks and deception."

Danielle joined him at the railing, passing a steaming espresso into his hands. "Just like our marriage." She smiled, softening the words. "Though we're finally wearing the same masks after all these years."

Sam studied her face, still marveling at how far they'd come since that traumatic discovery in 2011. "If Marcus planned this since I was nineteen, he couldn't have known I'd find you. That wasn't in his calculations."

"Families with certain aptitudes find each other," Danielle quoted, echoing Riccardo's words from Frosolone. "Maybe we were inevitable, despite everything we've been through."

Sam's phone vibrated with an encrypted message. He glanced at the screen, tension returning to his shoulders. "Roshkov confirms the timetable. The Venice Sphere will be moved tomorrow morning. Tonight is our only window."

"Then we'd better make it count," Danielle replied, her gaze shifting to the distant silhouette of Murano Island across the lagoon. "How much does Cade know?"

"More than we realized," Sam said. "His algorithm identified secondary security protocols we would have missed. He's already modified the access sequence."

Danielle nodded, a mother's pride mixing with operational concern. "The question isn't whether they're involved, but whether they're prepared. They've lived with this reality their entire lives, even if they didn't fully understand it at first."

Sam watched a water taxi navigate the morning traffic, each vessel moving according to unwritten rules that maintained the delicate balance of Venetian water transit. "Let's hope all of us are."

The Canal Grande Hotel's lobby hummed with late-afternoon activity as Sam and Danielle made their final preparations, discreetly checking equipment while maintaining their cover as anniversary celebrants preparing for Venice's most exclusive summer event.

"Signor Clayton," the concierge approached with practiced discretion, "your package has arrived from the restoration atelier."

Sam accepted the long rectangular box bearing the name of a renowned Venetian artisan. "Grazie. My wife has been looking forward to this."

Once back in their suite, Danielle secured the door while Sam opened the package on the antique writing desk. Inside lay two exquisite Venetian masks – a traditional black bauta with gilded edges for Sam and an elaborate volto design accented with sapphire and silver for Danielle. Beneath them rested a vintage leather folio containing detailed schematics of the Murano facility's security systems.

"Roshkov's information is consistent with what Cade found," Sam said, spreading the documents across the bed. "The Venice Sphere is housed in a temperature-controlled vault beneath the main furnace room."

Danielle studied the plans, her finger tracing possible infiltration routes with the practiced eye of someone who'd been part of these operations for over a decade. "The architectural design is practically medieval despite the modern security. They're using the original foundation structures from the sixteenth century."

"Which creates vulnerabilities the electronic systems can't fully compensate for," Sam added. "There's a maintenance access point here," he indicated a narrow passage, "with only secondary monitoring."

"And during the masquerade, half their security team will be at La Fenice providing protection for consortium members," Danielle concluded.

Sam's phone chirped with another encrypted message. He scanned it quickly, his expression darkening. "Kessler arrived this morning. He's personally overseeing the final inspection before tomorrow's transfer."

"Do we abort?" Danielle asked, already calculating alternative approaches with the efficiency she'd developed since her first significant field operation in Barbados.

Sam shook his head. "We proceed. His presence actually helps – he'll be attending the ball, which puts him away from Murano during our window."

The subtle chime of Sam's watch indicated an incoming secure communication. He activated the receiver discreetly built into his wedding band, hearing Cade's voice clearly despite the thousands of miles separating them.

"You're looking at outdated schematics," Cade said without preamble. "They've added frequency-shifting thermal sensors within the last twenty-four hours."

Sam exchanged glances with Danielle. "Can you bypass them?"

"Already done," Cade replied, professional confidence replacing his usual youthful enthusiasm. "I'm sending modified protocols to your secure drive now. You'll have a seven-minute window during the system's automated integrity check at exactly 11:42 PM."

"Seven minutes," Sam repeated, calculating transit times between La Fenice and Murano. "Cutting it close."

"It's all we've got," Cade said. "The system's too integrated for a longer disruption without triggering redundancies."

Sam heard keyboard clicks through the connection, followed by Cade's lowered voice. "Dad, there's something else. I've been analyzing communication patterns between security teams. Roshkov's movements don't match standard protocols."

"Meaning?"

"Either he's improvising extensively, or..."

"Or this is a trap," Sam finished. The possibility had haunted him since Copenhagen, the question of Roshkov's true allegiance remaining unresolved through fifteen years of intermittent contact.

"Be careful," Cade said, his professional demeanor momentarily giving way to the concern of a son who'd grown up understanding the dangers his parents faced.

"Always am."

After ending the communication, Sam turned to find Danielle already changing into the elegant midnight blue gown they'd purchased in Rome. Its classic styling concealed specialized pockets and reinforcements while maintaining the appearance of haute couture.

"Roshkov is playing his own game," Sam said. "Always has been."

Danielle pinned her hair up, revealing the graceful line of her neck. "The question is whether his game aligns with ours. After thirteen years of limited information, I still don't completely trust his motives."

"Guess we'll find out tonight," Sam replied, reaching for his tuxedo. As he dressed, he noted Danielle slipping a narrow ceramic blade into a hidden sheath built into her evening bag. After thirty years together—with thirteen of those years rebuilding trust after the revelation in 2011—they were finally seeing each other's complete selves, not just as partners in family life but as equals in this shadow world.

"Whatever happens tonight," Sam said, adjusting his cufflinks with their concealed lock picks, "I've never felt more married to you than I do right now. I know it's taken us years to get here..."

Danielle smiled, the expression transforming her operational focus into something profoundly intimate. "No more separate worlds—finally. We earned this partnership the hard way."

La Fenice Opera House blazed with light as Venice's elite arrived for the annual historical masquerade, a tradition dating back centuries though interrupted by periods of war and the opera house's multiple reconstructions after fires. Its current incarnation maintained the classical horseshoe design with five levels of ornate boxes surrounding the stage where musicians played Vivaldi's "Four Seasons" to establish the evening's refined atmosphere.

Sam and Danielle ascended the marble staircase, their masks in place, joining the elegant procession of disguised attendees. Despite the fanciful costumes, Sam easily identified at least seven security personnel strategically positioned throughout the main hall, their practiced stillness betraying their function.

"Kessler is in the director's box," Danielle murmured, her gaze flicking briefly toward the prime location above stage right. "With two associates."

Sam nodded almost imperceptibly, guiding her toward the champagne service. "Roshkov?"

"Not yet visible."

They circulated methodically, Sam establishing their presence as legitimate guests while Danielle mapped the security positions. The evening progressed according to ancient protocol – music, champagne, the formal promenade where couples displayed their costumes, followed by the opening dance in the adjoining ballroom.

Sam checked his watch. 10:18 PM. They needed to maintain their cover for another forty minutes before slipping away during the midnight buffet. As he calculated their extraction route, a tall figure in a plague doctor mask approached, the distinctive curved beak and crystal eye coverings concealing the wearer's identity.

"Dostoevsky had much to say about the human capacity for deception," the figure said in Roshkov's unmistakable cadence. "Would you agree, Professor Clayton?"

"I've always found him rather pessimistic," Sam replied, completing the recognition exchange established in Copenhagen fifteen years earlier.

Roshkov inclined his masked head slightly. "Walk with me. Both of you."

They followed him to a secluded alcove behind one of the massive velvet curtains, partially hidden from the main hall but with clear sightlines to Kessler's position.

"Your timetable has accelerated," Roshkov said without preamble. "Kessler has ordered the Venice Sphere moved tonight, not tomorrow. The transport team arrives at 1 AM."

Sam maintained his composure despite the surge of adrenaline. "Why tell us?"

"The enemy of my enemy makes for complex allegiances," Roshkov replied. "Your extraction plan is compromised. Three operatives are already positioned at your hotel awaiting your return."

"And we should trust this information why?" Danielle asked, her voice neutral. Years of operational experience had taught her when to challenge intelligence directly.

Roshkov turned toward her, the plague doctor mask creating an unsettling effect as he tilted his head. "Because, Mrs. Clayton, I've been working against Kessler from within since before Copenhagen. You've been part of this longer than you realize."

Sam studied the man's body language, searching for tells beneath the elaborate costume. "You work for Kessler. You're Director of Strategic Resources for his entire operation."

"Positions are not the same as allegiances," Roshkov said. "Your recruitment wasn't Marcus's initiative, Mr. Clayton. It was your father's design from the beginning."

The statement hit Sam like a physical blow. "Carmichael?"

"The saxophone continues playing between the notes," Roshkov said softly. "Your father understood that some operations require generations to come to fruition."

Danielle placed her hand on Sam's arm, steadying him as she had done through countless crises since their first painful confrontation in 2011. "If what you're saying is true, why reveal yourself now?"

"Because tonight everything changes," Roshkov replied. "The Venice Sphere contains more than evidence of climate data manipulation. It holds the complete operational structure of the Consortium, including the council to whom Kessler himself answers."

"Council?" Sam questioned, reassessing fifteen years of intelligence on Kessler's organization.

"Twelve individuals whose combined wealth exceeds the GDP of most nations," Roshkov explained. "Kessler is merely their most visible instrument."

"And your role in all this?" Danielle pressed, her years of partial operational knowledge making her particularly attuned to inconsistencies.

"Let's just say there are entities with longer memories and deeper patience than even the Consortium," Roshkov said. "I was placed within Kessler's organization twenty-three years ago with very specific objectives."

"By whom?" Sam demanded.

Roshkov checked his watch, an anachronistic detail against his historical costume. "Questions for another time. You have fifty-eight minutes before the vault transport team arrives. I've arranged access to the private water entrance used for art deliveries."

He handed Sam a small device resembling an antique pocket watch. "This will bypass the biometric requirements for the main vault. The secondary protocols your son identified remain your challenge."

Sam examined the device skeptically. "Why help us now?"

"Because you and your family have earned it," Roshkov said. "And because Marcus would be disappointed if I didn't honor our arrangement."

Before Sam could respond, Roshkov glanced over his shoulder. "Kessler is moving. I'll create a diversion at 11:30. Use the service corridor behind the director's office for your exit."

With a slight bow more befitting the historical period of his costume than modern interaction, Roshkov melted back into the crowd, leaving Sam and Danielle to process this dramatic shift in their operational understanding.

"If he's telling the truth," Danielle said, "our entire timeline is compressed."

Sam nodded, already recalculating. "We need to contact Cade. If the Sphere is being moved tonight, we need updated security protocols."

They moved casually toward the grand staircase, maintaining their cover while Sam activated his concealed communication device. The encrypted connection took several seconds to establish before Cade's voice came through the small receiver.

"I was about to contact you," Cade said immediately. "There's unusual activity at the Murano facility. Power usage spiked in the last twenty minutes, and they've activated additional security protocols."

"They're moving the Sphere tonight," Sam confirmed. "We need to accelerate. Can you adjust the bypass to give us access before midnight?"

Keyboard clicks sounded through the connection as Cade worked. "I can create a new window at 11:38, but it reduces your access time to five minutes."

"We'll manage," Sam said. "Roshkov provided a bypass device for the biometrics."

"Roshkov?" Cade's voice sharpened. "Dad, every analysis I've run shows him as a primary Consortium asset."

"Every good operative maintains their cover," Sam replied. "Just like your grandfather apparently did with me."

A brief silence followed. "What are you talking about?"

"Later," Sam promised. "Focus on getting us that window."

"Working on it," Cade said, his tone shifting back to operational focus. "But something feels wrong about this timing."

Sam and Danielle exchanged glances, the same concern evident in both their expressions. "Trust nothing, verify everything," Sam said, echoing one of Marcus's earliest lessons.

"Access codes updated," Cade confirmed after a moment. "11:38 sharp. The system will give you exactly five minutes before integrity protocols trigger. Mom, Dad... be careful."

"We will," Danielle said. "Love you, Cade."

When the connection ended, they positioned themselves near the service corridor, timing the security rotations. The ornate clock above the main staircase showed 11:22 PM.

"Thoughts?" Sam asked, knowing Danielle would catch his meaning.

"If Roshkov is setting a trap, it's elaborate even by his standards," she replied. "The information about the transport team feels genuine, but the revelation about Carmichael orchestrating your recruitment..."

"Feels like emotional manipulation," Sam finished.

Danielle nodded. "Designed to throw you off balance during a critical operation. After thirteen years of working alongside you, I've learned to recognize when someone's trying to manipulate us."

"Then we proceed with extreme caution," Sam decided. "And trust nothing Roshkov hasn't personally demonstrated."

At precisely 11:30, a commotion erupted at the main entrance. Several security personnel moved quickly in that direction as voices rose in alarm. Through the shifting crowd, Sam glimpsed Roshkov's plague doctor mask near a service entrance, the Russian making a subtle gesture toward the corridor behind the director's office.

"That's our cue," Sam said.

They moved smoothly through the crowd, the anonymity of their masks providing perfect cover as they slipped into the designated corridor. The service passageway curved behind the historic opera house's administrative sections, eventually leading to a small dock where deliveries arrived via the canal.

A vintage wooden Riva awaited, its engine idling quietly. The boat appeared to be a standard luxury water taxi, but Sam immediately noted the modified engine housing and reinforced hull – this was no ordinary vessel.

"Your transportation, Mr. and Mrs. Clayton," said a young man in traditional gondolier attire. "Courtesy of a mutual friend."

Sam helped Danielle aboard before joining her, keeping his movements natural despite his heightened vigilance. As the boat pulled away from La Fenice's service dock, Sam scanned the canal banks for surveillance, finding nothing obvious but assuming they were being monitored regardless.

"Murano in twelve minutes," the driver said, opening the throttle as they entered a less congested channel. "You'll find equipment under the rear seat."

Sam retrieved a waterproof bag containing additional tools – glass cutters, thermal suppressors, and a specialized scanner for detecting electronic tripwires. The equipment was top-grade and precisely what they needed, increasing Sam's unease about Roshkov's apparent cooperation.

"Still feels like we're walking into something," Danielle murmured, adjusting her evening gown to allow greater freedom of movement.

"Probably because we are," Sam replied. "But the Venice Sphere is worth the risk."

The boat curved around the northern lagoon, the lights of Venice proper receding as they approached Murano's silhouette. Unlike the main islands with their tourist-filled waterfronts, Murano's shoreline appeared industrial and largely deserted at this hour, the famous glass factories silent until morning.

Their driver reduced speed as they approached a small, unmarked dock extending from an ancient brick building. "Loading entrance," he explained.

"Used for art shipments and materials too delicate for the main cargo areas."

He guided the Riva alongside the weathered wooden pier with practiced precision. "I'll wait fifteen minutes. After that, you're on your own."

Sam checked his watch: 11:34 PM. Four minutes until Cade's access window opened. They disembarked silently, Danielle removing her heeled shoes as they crossed the wooden planking to a heavy iron door.

Roshkov's device bypassed the electronic lock with a soft click. Inside, they found themselves in a dimly lit receiving area, surrounded by crates of raw materials and finished glass art pieces awaiting shipment. Sam activated the thermal suppressor, creating a bubble of ambient temperature around them to defeat heat sensors.

"Server room is two levels down," Sam whispered, indicating a spiral staircase descending into darkness. "Cade's window opens in two minutes."

They moved efficiently through the silent facility, their formal attire incongruous against the industrial backdrop of furnaces and workshop equipment. The spiral staircase led to a modern security door

embedded incongruously in the ancient stone wall –
the physical barrier between the glass factory's
public face and its clandestine purpose.

Sam checked his watch again: 11:37 PM. Sixty
seconds until their window. He positioned Roshkov's
device against the biometric panel, watching the
small display flicker as it processed the security
protocols.

The moment his watch displayed 11:38, the security
panel emitted a soft tone and the reinforced door
unlocked with a pneumatic hiss. They entered
swiftly, finding themselves in a state-of-the-art
server facility, the temperature noticeably cooler as
climate control systems maintained optimal
conditions for the sensitive equipment.

"Five minutes," Sam reminded Danielle as they
navigated between server racks toward the central
storage vault indicated in Roshkov's schematics.

The vault itself presented as a glass cube in the
center of the server room, its transparent walls
revealing nothing of the security measures
protecting it. Inside, mounted on an illuminated
pedestal, sat what appeared to be an exquisite piece
of Murano glasswork – a perfect sphere of swirling

blue and green, its surface embedded with flecks of gold.

"The Venice Sphere," Danielle whispered, approaching the glass cube cautiously.

Sam consulted the scanner, confirming what Cade had reported. "Multiple layers of security, but the primary systems are temporarily bypassed. Secondary protocols active but suppressed for system diagnostics."

He placed Roshkov's device against the cube's access panel, watching as complex algorithmic patterns scrolled across its small display. After what felt like an eternity but was merely thirty seconds, the cube's door silently swung open.

"Three minutes remaining," Danielle said, checking her watch as Sam carefully approached the pedestal.

The Sphere itself appeared deceptively simple – a masterpiece of glassblowing art that would fetch a premium price in any gallery. But Sam knew its true value lay in the quantum data storage technology embedded within the glass matrix itself, containing terabytes of encrypted information documenting decades of Consortium operations.

Following Cade's instructions, Sam removed a specialized transfer device from his equipment bag, placing it carefully against the Sphere's surface. The device adhered silently, its display indicating the beginning of the data extraction process.

"Two minutes," Danielle warned, positioned near the door to monitor for approaching threats.

Sam watched the transfer progress indicator with growing tension, the specialized device copying the Sphere's contents while leaving the original intact – evidence of their intrusion would only be detected during detailed analysis.

"Almost there," Sam said. "Ninety seconds remaining."

The transfer device chimed softly, signaling completion. Sam carefully removed it from the Sphere and secured it in an inner pocket of his tuxedo jacket. He had just stepped back from the pedestal when the vault's lighting shifted subtly.

"Sam," Danielle's voice carried new urgency. "We have company."

Through the server room's glass doors, they spotted two security personnel approaching from the stairwell, moving with purpose rather than alarm – a routine check rather than response to an intrusion.

"One minute until system reset," Sam noted. "We need a diversion."

Danielle reached into her evening bag, removing what appeared to be a compact mirror. "Northeast corner, behind the auxiliary cooling system. Forty seconds."

Sam understood immediately. They retreated from the vault, securing its door behind them, and positioned themselves behind the designated server rack just as Danielle activated the device. Across the room, a small electromagnetic pulse disrupted the monitoring systems, triggering emergency protocols that directed security toward that location.

As the guards diverted to investigate the apparent system malfunction, Sam and Danielle slipped toward the exit, timing their movements between security camera sweeps. They reached the stairwell with fifteen seconds remaining before system reset, ascending rapidly toward the main floor.

"Exit through the furnace room," Sam directed, recalling the facility layout from Roshkov's schematics. "Loading dock will be watched now."

They navigated through the darkened workshop, the massive glass furnaces dormant overnight creating eerie shadows across the ancient brick walls. An employee exit provided their escape route, opening onto a small side canal where water taxis occasionally delivered workers.

"Boat's gone," Danielle observed as they emerged onto the canal side. "As expected."

Sam nodded, already assessing alternatives. "Secondary extraction point is northeast, past the showroom."

They moved silently along the canal edge, still in their formal attire but with masks removed for better visibility. The Venice Sphere data transfer device felt heavy in Sam's pocket, the culmination of years of investigation finally secured.

As they rounded the corner of the main showroom building, Sam spotted a familiar silhouette on a small dock ahead – the plague doctor mask unmistakable even in the dim light.

"Right on schedule," Roshkov said as they approached. "I trust the acquisition was successful?"

"Why are you still here?" Sam demanded, maintaining distance between them. "Your role was to create a diversion at La Fenice."

"And so I did," Roshkov replied, removing his mask to reveal his pale features in the moonlight. "But I wanted to ensure the transfer completed successfully. Kessler's transport team arrives in twenty minutes."

"Our extraction?" Danielle asked, her posture indicating readiness for potential conflict.

Roshkov gestured toward a small, unmarked boat moored at the dock. "This will take you to a safe house on Giudecca. Italian intelligence will meet you there for debriefing."

Sam studied Roshkov carefully. "You're not coming."

"My position within the Consortium remains valuable," Roshkov explained. "Tonight will be attributed to external operators, possibly Interpol. My cover remains intact."

"If you're truly working against Kessler," Sam pressed, "why not expose him now? Come with us, provide testimony."

Roshkov smiled thinly. "Because Kessler is merely a symptom, not the disease. The council remains largely untouched by tonight's action."

"Then why help us at all?" Danielle asked, drawing on her years of operational intuition.

"Consider it an investment in the future," Roshkov said. "Your children have remarkable talents, Mr. and Mrs. Clayton. The next generation often succeeds where ours has failed."

Sam felt a chill at the mention of his children. "Stay away from my family."

"On the contrary," Roshkov replied, "I've been protecting them for years. Ask Marcus about Copenhagen sometime – about who diverted the team sent to surveil your home while you were away."

Before Sam could respond, distant voices carried across the water – security personnel beginning wider search patterns from the facility.

"Time to go," Roshkov said, gesturing toward the waiting boat. "The data you've acquired will expose Kessler's operations but not the full extent of the Consortium's reach. That requires additional work."

"By whom?" Sam demanded. "Who are you really working for?"

Roshkov replaced his mask, once again becoming the anonymous plague doctor. "The same entity your father served, Mr. Clayton. Though perhaps with greater awareness than Carmichael initially had."

He pressed a small envelope into Sam's hand. "Coordinates for your next steps. Marcus will understand their significance."

With unexpected swiftness, Roshkov turned and disappeared into the shadows between buildings, leaving Sam and Danielle alone on the dock as the security team's voices grew closer.

"We need to move," Danielle urged, already moving toward the extraction boat.

Sam pocketed the envelope and joined her, his mind racing with implications. As they pulled away from Murano, navigating toward the dark silhouette of Giudecca across the lagoon, the lights of Venice glittered like stars fallen to earth – beautiful, distant, and cold.

"If Roshkov is telling the truth," Sam said quietly, "everything we believed about my recruitment, about Carmichael's role..."

"Your father was a remarkable man," Danielle said, placing her hand over his. "Whatever his involvement, whatever path led us here – we built something real together, Sam. Even through those difficult years after I discovered the truth."

Sam nodded, watching Venice recede as their boat sliced through the dark waters. "No more separate worlds. Finally, after all this time."

The Venice Sphere data secure against his chest represented the culmination of years of work, yet somehow felt like merely the beginning of a larger revelation. Behind them, lights flooded the Murano facility as Kessler's transport team discovered the intrusion, too late to prevent the extraction of their most closely guarded secrets.

Sam thought of Cade halfway across the world, his technical brilliance providing the crucial access. Of Ellie and Rae pursuing their specialized paths, each developing talents that mirrored yet transformed their parents' capabilities. Of Mackie, youngest but perhaps most perceptive, seeing patterns others missed.

"Whatever brought us together," Danielle said, as though reading his thoughts, "what we built is ours,

Sam. The family we created, the life we shared—
even with the strain and distance after 2011—those
are real."

"Not destined," Sam replied, reaching for her hand.
"Just prepared."

The lights of Giudecca grew closer, their safe harbor
awaiting with Italian intelligence contacts and
secure communications to share their acquisition.
But Sam knew the night's true significance lay not in
the data they'd stolen, but in the revelation that his
entire life – from college recruitment to marriage to
children – might have been orchestrated as part of a
multi-generational intelligence operation.

As their boat docked at the private marina on
Giudecca's northern shore, Sam made a decision.
Whatever game Carmichael had been playing,
whatever role Marcus and Roshkov had in his life's
path, the family he and Danielle had built
transcended any operational design. Their children
weren't assets or experiments – they were people
making their own choices, developing their own
talents.

"Maybe we're stronger together than separated by secrets," Sam said, helping Danielle onto the dock where their contact waited.

"No more separate worlds," she affirmed, squeezing his hand as they stepped forward to complete their mission, the Venice Sphere's secrets finally theirs to reveal.

Chapter 10
Final Exposure
August 2024

Sam pressed his palm against the cool stone balustrade overlooking Florence's ancient skyline. The morning mist clung to the Arno River below, shrouding Ponte Vecchio's weathered arches. Three days had passed since their narrow escape from Venice with the Venice Sphere data securely extracted, and exhaustion creased the corners of his eyes.

"Beautiful, isn't it?" Danielle joined him, slipping her hand into his with the easy familiarity they'd recently reclaimed after years of careful distance. "Hard to believe something so enduring could exist in a world where truth seems so... malleable."

Sam squeezed her hand, grateful for how far they'd come since the fracture that began in 2011. "Maybe that's why they built it to last. Someone has to bear witness."

The extraction had succeeded beyond their expectations. With Roshkov's unexpected assistance and Cade's remote support breaking through the facility's security protocols during the Masquerade Ball, they'd managed to copy the Venice Sphere data while leaving the original intact—a perfect infiltration. The delay in discovery had given them precious time to analyze its contents before determining their next steps.

"Phillips confirmed the rendezvous. We meet his team at the Boboli Gardens at eleven." Sam's voice remained low despite their careful surveillance detection route that morning.

Danielle nodded, her scientific mind already working through the implications. "The data verification is proceeding faster than expected. Cade's algorithm identified authentication patterns that would have taken conventional analysis weeks to uncover."

"He's always seen patterns where others see chaos," Sam said, pride evident in his voice. "Just like his mother."

Danielle smiled, though a different concern shadowed her eyes than in years past. "I've been thinking about what happens after. When this is over. Will it ever truly be over, Sam?"

Before he could answer, his secure phone vibrated. A text from their Italian intelligence contact: Operation Moonlight Sonata was proceeding to phase two.

"Time to go," he said, guiding her away from the vista. "The world's about to change."

The Boboli Gardens sprawled behind Palazzo Pitti like a verdant labyrinth. Sam and Danielle followed the gravel path past elaborate fountains and precisely trimmed hedges, staying within sight of other tourists while maintaining operational awareness. They'd chosen lightweight linen clothing appropriate for August tourism, with Sam's specialized equipment concealed in a photographer's vest.

Phillips waited at the Amphitheater, a semicircular space surrounded by ancient statues. American-born but with dual Italian citizenship, he'd served as their primary liaison to multiple intelligence agencies since Rome.

"The preliminary analysis exceeded expectations," Phillips said without preamble, falling into step beside them. "Four independent teams have verified the data integrity. It's unequivocally authentic."

"And the content?" Danielle asked, her years of limited operational involvement having honed her focus for the essential questions.

"More damning than anticipated." Phillips guided them toward a secluded alcove shielded by cypress trees. "We've identified direct financial ties between Kessler and nine sovereign wealth funds manipulating commodity prices based on falsified climate projections. The manipulated data created artificial scarcity where none existed and masked actual environmental concerns that would have affected resource pricing."

Sam nodded grimly. "Perfect information asymmetry. They see the real data, act on it privately, while feeding manipulated projections to governments and markets."

"Precisely. The Venice Sphere contained the complete authentication chain—every falsified report, who authorized it, who implemented it, and who profited." Phillips handed Sam a secure tablet. "We've prepared a comprehensive briefing for your review before tomorrow's symposium."

The tablet displayed a complex network of shell companies, data manipulation points, and resource acquisition patterns spanning three decades. At the center sat Kessler, connected to twelve individuals identified only by encryption keys.

"The Council," Sam said quietly.

"Yes. We've identified eight of the twelve already. Heads of sovereign wealth funds, energy conglomerates, private equity firms specializing in water rights and agricultural land." Phillips swiped to another screen. "Your son's analysis proved instrumental. His algorithm recognized the fractal pattern linking seemingly unrelated manipulation points."

Danielle studied the data, her scientific training immediately recognizing the elegance of the deception. "They weren't just falsifying data—they were creating an entirely parallel climate narrative, one that served their financial interests while ignoring actual environmental concerns."

"Controlling the narrative to control the resources," Sam said. "How soon can we move to public disclosure?"

"That's why we're meeting. The international climate symposium at Rome's EUR Convention Center begins tomorrow. Dr. Lars Johannsen has agreed to present the findings during his keynote address."

Sam recognized the name immediately. "The Institute of Climate Change director? That gives the findings immense credibility."

"Precisely why we approached him. He's spent years questioning anomalies in climate databases, but never had proof of systematic manipulation. Now he does." Phillips lowered his voice further. "We've arranged a secure video connection for your son to participate remotely in the technical verification panel. His algorithm is central to understanding how the manipulation remained undetected for decades."

Danielle tensed slightly, the protective instinct that had guided her through thirteen years of managing family security while maintaining emotional distance from Sam surfacing again. "Is that wise? Exposing him publicly?"

"We've considered that," Phillips assured her. "His participation will be anonymous, introduced only as 'Technical Analyst C.' No name, no identifying details. But his testimony on the mathematical patterns is crucial for credibility."

Sam exchanged a look with Danielle, their silent communication perfected despite the years of emotional barriers between them. Their son was already involved—had been since birth, according to what they'd learned about Carmichael's long-term planning. The question wasn't whether to protect him through isolation anymore, but how to embrace his role while minimizing risk.

"I'll speak with him," Sam decided. "It's his choice to make."

As they continued walking through the gardens, Phillips outlined the symposium security arrangements. "We're coordinating with multiple agencies for the public disclosure. Once the information is released, there's no putting it back in the box."

"What about Kessler?" Danielle asked, her voice carrying the weight of someone who had spent years calculating threats to her family.

"We're tracking his movements. Currently in Geneva, presumably meeting with financial backers. Our analysis suggests he'll attempt to distance himself, claiming to be a victim of manipulation by subordinates."

Sam shook his head. "He's too thorough for that. He'll have contingencies."

"Which is why we need yours as well," Phillips responded, handing Sam a small encrypted drive. "This contains emergency extraction protocols if needed. Memorize and destroy." He checked his watch. "Our next meeting is at Pisa tomorrow morning before proceeding to Rome. The botanical garden provides excellent surveillance protection."

As Phillips departed, taking a different path to avoid association, Sam turned to Danielle. "Ready for the next phase?"

Her eyes reflected determination and the weight of everything they'd endured since that traumatic discovery in 2011. "The fact that our family was targeted because of abilities Carmichael identified generations ago still feels... unsettling. But I'm beyond ready to expose what they've done."

Sam nodded, tucking the encrypted drive securely into his vest. "Then let's get to work."

The Orto Botanico di Pisa, one of the world's oldest botanical gardens, offered natural surveillance advantages with its ordered pathways and carefully tended specimens. Sam and Danielle arrived early, using the peaceful morning hours to detect any unusual surveillance patterns before their scheduled meeting.

"I spoke with Cade last night," Sam said quietly as they examined a collection of medicinal plants. "He's agreed to provide technical testimony, though I can tell he's processing the implications of how central his algorithm has become."

"And how do you feel about it?" Danielle studied her husband's face, reading him with the clarity that thirteen years of operational partnership—if not always emotional closeness—had given her. "Your father orchestrated your recruitment, apparently anticipated our children's capabilities, and set all this in motion decades ago."

Sam's jaw tightened momentarily—the subtle tell Danielle had recognized since early in their marriage. "I've been asking myself if anything was real. My career choice, meeting you, our life together—was it all part of some grand intelligence design?"

"You know better than that," Danielle said firmly, stopping to face him directly. "Whatever brought us together, what we built is ours. The family we created, the life we shared—those are real, Sam. Even when we were most broken after 2011, that truth remained."

Before he could respond, a familiar figure approached along the garden path. Ivan Roshkov moved with his characteristic fluid grace, dressed impeccably in a light summer suit despite the morning heat.

"The medicinal garden is particularly fascinating this time of year," Roshkov said by way of greeting, his ice-blue eyes scanning the surroundings continuously. "Ancient remedies sometimes prove more effective than modern solutions."

Sam maintained his composed exterior despite his surprise. "I didn't expect to see you here. Aren't you concerned about exposure after Venice?"

"Positions are not the same as allegiances, Mr. Clayton." Roshkov gestured toward a more secluded bench beneath a sprawling magnolia. "I believe we have matters to discuss before your symposium appearance."

Once seated, Roshkov produced a small device that emitted a subtle electronic hum—counter-surveillance technology. "We have approximately four minutes of security," he said. "I'll be direct. The Council is aware of the Venice Sphere compromise."

Sam tensed. "How?"

"I informed them," Roshkov said calmly. "Or rather, I informed them that an attempt had been made, but assured them it was unsuccessful. This gives us time, but not much."

"Why would you help us?" Danielle asked, her analytical mind assessing his possible motivations with the precision she'd developed through years of operational awareness.

"Our objectives temporarily align." Roshkov's thin lips formed what might have been a smile. "The Council has grown... complacent. Kessler's climate manipulation strategy was brilliant initially but has become increasingly reckless."

"So this is an internal power struggle," Sam concluded.

"In part. But my primary allegiance remains as it always has been—to the same entity your father served."

Sam felt Danielle's hand tighten around his. "And what entity is that?"

"One that values balance over dominance." Roshkov checked his watch. "Two minutes remaining. What matters now is this: Kessler will not be at the symposium, but he's directed resources to disrupt it. The evidence you present will be attacked as fraudulent. You need credible, public verification from multiple sources."

"We've arranged that," Sam said. "Independent climate scientists, data forensics experts—"

"You need someone from inside," Roshkov interrupted. "I can provide that verification. A senior Consortium member publicly confirming the authenticity of the data would be... compelling."

Sam studied the Russian carefully. "At significant personal risk."

"As I said, positions change. Allegiances endure." Roshkov stood as his device emitted a warning tone. "One final piece of information. Maria Rossi is secure. The operation in Ukraine has been neutralized."

Danielle inhaled sharply. "My mother? How do you —"

"All in due time, Mrs. Clayton." Roshkov pocketed his device. "I'll see you both in Rome tomorrow. Do transmit my regards to your son—his fractal algorithm is quite remarkable."

As Roshkov walked away, disappearing among a tour group of Japanese visitors, Sam and Danielle exchanged concerned glances.

"Can we trust him?" Danielle asked, the wariness in her voice reflecting years of learning to navigate Sam's world of shifting allegiances and hidden agendas.

"Partially, maybe. But we'll have contingencies in place." Sam stood, offering his hand. "We should move. Our train to Rome leaves in ninety minutes."

The FAO Headquarters in Rome, housed in a striking modern complex near the Circus Maximus, served as their final preparation point before tomorrow's symposium. International climate scientists had gathered for pre-conference verification of the Venice Sphere data, providing an ideal cover for the Claytons' meeting with key intelligence partners.

Dr. Lars Johannsen greeted them warmly in a secured conference room. The distinguished climate scientist's reputation for integrity made him the perfect public face for tomorrow's revelations.

"The verification process is complete," Johannsen confirmed, his Danish accent pronounced but his English precise. "Three independent teams have confirmed both the authenticity of the data and the systematic nature of the manipulations."

On the large display screen, Cade appeared via secure video link, his expression serious but confident. At eighteen, he already demonstrated remarkable poise explaining complex technical concepts—a young man who had grown up understanding far more about his parents' secret world than most children.

"The manipulation pattern follows a fractal encryption methodology," Cade explained, sharing his screen to display mathematical models. "It's beautiful, in a disturbing way. Like a Bach fugue composed of falsified data."

Sam felt a surge of pride watching his son command the attention of scientists twice his age. Cade continued, "By minimizing historical variations, current changes seem more dramatic—or less so—depending on what narrative you wish to create."

"Precisely," Johannsen agreed. "The Consortium has been playing a generations-long game. By establishing false baselines and selectively emphasizing or minimizing certain climate patterns, they've created information advantage in resource markets worth trillions."

The technical discussion continued, with Cade demonstrating how his algorithm had identified manipulation signatures across decades of climate records. When complete, Phillips activated additional security protocols for the final briefing.

"Tomorrow's disclosure is coordinated across multiple platforms," he explained. "Dr. Johannsen's keynote will present the scientific evidence, followed by technical verification from independent experts including Analyst C." He nodded toward Cade's video feed. "Simultaneous press releases to major media outlets will establish the financial connections. And financial regulators in seven countries will announce investigations into market manipulation based on falsified environmental data."

"And Roshkov?" Sam asked.

"His offer to provide insider verification is... unexpected but potentially valuable. We've arranged appropriate security, though his true motivations remain unclear."

As the meeting concluded, Sam requested a private moment with Cade while Danielle discussed scientific details with Johannsen. When the room cleared, Sam studied his son's image on the screen.

"You've done remarkable work," he said. "But tomorrow changes everything. Once this goes public —"

"I know, Dad." Cade's expression reflected maturity beyond his years—the maturity of a child raised with security protocols and careful awareness. "I've been thinking about what this means for all of us. Especially after learning about Grandpa's involvement in... well, everything."

"Does it bother you? Learning that your talents might have been anticipated, even... cultivated?"

Cade considered the question carefully. "Not destined. Prepared. There's a difference." He adjusted his camera slightly. "Besides, maybe we're stronger together than separated by secrets."

Sam smiled, recognizing the wisdom in his son's perspective and hearing an echo of what Danielle had argued for since their confrontation in Paris five years ago. "Whatever brought us to this point, what matters is what we choose to do now. You sure you're ready for tomorrow?"

"As ready as any of us can be." Cade's expression grew serious again. "Have you considered what comes after? When the Consortium is exposed?"

"One battle at a time," Sam reminded him. "Focus on tomorrow. We'll address whatever comes next together."

After disconnecting, Sam rejoined Danielle as they prepared to leave for their hotel. The anticipation of tomorrow's revelations hung between them, along with the unspoken acknowledgment of how far they'd come in rebuilding what had fractured thirteen years ago.

"Whatever comes next," Danielle said, echoing his words to Cade, "we face it together. No more separate worlds—just as I've wanted since Paris."

The EUR Convention Center buzzed with energy as the International Climate Data Integrity Symposium began. Originally planned as a specialized academic conference, attendance had swelled overnight as rumors circulated about significant revelations. Security had been discreetly enhanced, with plainclothes personnel positioned throughout the modernist complex.

Sam and Danielle sat in the third row, positioned for optimal visibility while maintaining evacuation options. Around them, climate scientists and policy experts from around the world settled in as Dr. Johannsen approached the podium.

"For twenty years," Johannsen began, his voice commanding immediate attention, "I have dedicated my career to understanding climate patterns and their implications for humanity's future. Today, I must share disturbing evidence that the very foundation of climate science has been compromised."

The room fell silent as Johannsen methodically presented the first evidence from the Venice Sphere data. Screens displayed comparison charts showing original climate measurements alongside manipulated versions that had entered official databases.

"The pattern of manipulation is neither random nor politically motivated as some might suspect," Johannsen continued. "Rather, it follows a sophisticated mathematical algorithm designed to create specific market advantages in resource allocation, particularly water rights, agricultural futures, and energy investments."

As Johannsen detailed the technical evidence, Sam observed the room carefully. Most scientists showed shock or growing anger, while a few—possibly Consortium-connected—appeared increasingly uncomfortable.

The presentation shifted to the technical verification panel, where Cade appeared via secure video as "Analyst C," his face partially obscured and voice slightly modified. With remarkable clarity, he explained the fractal pattern underlying decades of data manipulation.

"The encryption signature reveals authorization chains extending to the highest levels of what we now identify as the Consortium," Cade explained, displaying complex mathematical models. "Each manipulation required multiple authorizations, creating an accountability structure that we can now trace definitively."

As the technical presentation concluded, the symposium's focus shifted to the financial implications. International regulators detailed the beginning of coordinated investigations into market manipulation based on privileged access to accurate climate data while public markets operated on falsified projections.

Then came the moment Sam had been anticipating with uncertainty. Ivan Roshkov approached the podium, introducing himself as the former Director of Strategic Resources for Kessler Global Consulting.

"I appear before you today to confirm the authenticity of the evidence presented," Roshkov stated, his composed delivery creating a sensation throughout the hall. "For nearly fifteen years, I participated in what I believed was legitimate resource management strategy. The evidence you've seen today represents merely the visible portion of a comprehensive system designed to create market advantages through information asymmetry."

Cameras flashed and reporters hurriedly took notes as Roshkov methodically confirmed key aspects of the Consortium's operations. When he finished, the symposium erupted in questions. Sam noticed several attendees hurriedly leaving—likely Consortium-connected participants recognizing the catastrophic exposure unfolding.

Phillips appeared beside them as the question period continued. "Initial media coverage is exceeding expectations," he reported quietly. "Financial markets are already responding to the revelations. Several of the identified Council members have issued denials, but regulatory investigations have commenced in multiple jurisdictions."

"And Kessler?" Sam asked.

"No public statement yet. Our intelligence suggests he's activated contingency plans, likely attempting to distance himself from the evidence. But Roshkov's testimony makes that considerably more difficult."

As the symposium transitioned to break-out sessions analyzing specific aspects of the manipulation, Sam and Danielle stepped outside to a secured terrace overlooking Rome's EUR district. The clean modernist lines of the fascist-era architecture provided a strangely appropriate backdrop for the dismantling of another authoritarian structure—the Consortium's global manipulation system.

"It's really happening," Danielle said quietly. "After all these years."

Sam nodded, watching media vans arriving in growing numbers outside the convention center. "The Venice Sphere data is too comprehensive to dismiss. The authentication chains too clear. It will take time for the full implications to unfold, but the Consortium's information advantage is finished."

"And the children? Their involvement?"

"Cade's identity remains protected despite his contribution. The others were never directly exposed." Sam squeezed her hand. "I've been thinking about Marcus's message—about the next generation often succeeding where ours failed. Maybe this was always meant to be their fight as much as ours."

Before Danielle could respond, Phillips approached with urgent purpose. "We've received a secure transmission addressed specifically to you," he said, handing Sam a tablet. "It came through channels only Marcus Cartier would know."

The tablet displayed a brief video. Marcus appeared, looking remarkably unchanged despite his supposed death nearly two years earlier. His message was succinct:

"Sam, if you're seeing this, the Venice Sphere exposure has succeeded. Well done. But the Council remains largely untouched by today's action. They've been preparing contingencies for decades." Marcus's expression grew more serious. "There's more to this than climate data manipulation. The next phase begins at coordinates you'll recognize from Carmichael's Midnight Saxophone. The music continues between the notes, old friend."

As the video concluded, Sam felt the weight of realization. This success, while significant, represented only one battle in a longer campaign that had been unfolding across generations. And somehow, Carmichael had anticipated it all.

"What now?" Danielle asked, reading his expression with the accuracy that thirty years of marriage afforded—a connection that had persisted even through their most distant years.

Sam glanced at his watch as media coverage of the symposium's revelations spread across global networks. "Now we finish what we started here, then follow the music. Note by note, until we find all the pieces of the Venice Sphere."

As they turned to re-enter the convention center, Sam's secure phone vibrated with an incoming message from Cade: "Dad, something's happened. I've found another pattern in the data—something we missed. Call as soon as you can."

The next chapter was already beginning.

That evening, secluded in their Rome hotel suite after a day of historic revelations, Sam and Danielle reviewed the extraordinary events while preparing for their return home. The symposium had exceeded all expectations, with global media coverage of the Consortium's climate data manipulation dominating headlines worldwide.

"Financial markets are still processing the implications," Danielle said, scanning news reports on her tablet. "Trading has been temporarily suspended in companies directly linked to Kessler Global Consulting."

Sam nodded, his attention divided between the immediate aftermath and the deeper implications of Marcus's message. "Eight of the twelve Council members have been publicly identified. That's significant progress, but—"

"But Marcus implied they remain largely untouched," Danielle finished his thought, the years of operational partnership having attuned her to the subtext of intelligence communications. "What do you think he meant about there being 'more to this than climate data manipulation'?"

Before Sam could answer, his secure connection to Cade activated. Their son's face appeared, excited but controlled as he shared his screen displaying complex mathematical models.

"I found something embedded within the fractal pattern," Cade explained. "The climate data manipulation was hiding something else—a secondary encryption layer that appears completely unrelated to environmental information."

"What kind of information?" Sam asked, leaning closer to the screen.

"I'm not entirely sure yet, but it appears to be a comprehensive database of some kind. The encryption is unlike anything I've seen before." Cade's eyes showed the familiar intensity when tackling complex problems. "I think this is what Marcus was referring to—the climate operation was concealing something bigger."

Sam exchanged a significant look with Danielle. "Send what you have through the secure channel. We'll analyze it when we return."

After disconnecting, Sam stood by the window overlooking Rome's ancient skyline, illuminated against the night sky. Thirty years of teaching had cultivated his patience, but decades of intelligence work had taught him to recognize when patterns shifted fundamentally.

"We're going home," he told Danielle. "Whatever comes next, we face it together. As a family."

Danielle joined him at the window, her hand finding his with a warmth that spoke of their completed reconciliation after years of careful distance. "The next generation often succeeds where ours has failed," she echoed Marcus's words. "Our children have remarkable talents, Sam. Perhaps they're the ones who will follow the music to its conclusion."

As Rome's eternal lights glimmered below, Sam considered the coordinated forces his family had helped set in motion today—scientific, regulatory, journalistic, and intelligence. The Consortium's climate manipulation had been exposed, but

Marcus's warning suggested this victory was merely prelude.

The shadow war continued, but no longer in isolation. Whatever came next, they would face it together—no more separate worlds.

Chapter 11
Bye, Bye Blue
June 2025

"It's all of you," Sam muttered, staring at the photograph spread across his desk. "He knew it would be all of you."

The image showed his children at various ages - candid shots blended into a single composition - each captured in a moment of concentration: Ellie examining water samples, Rae translating texts in multiple languages, Cade working with complex algorithms, and even young Mackie sketching architectural details with uncanny precision.

The collage had been hidden in Carmichael's saxophone case, delivered yesterday exactly as specified in the will. Five months after his father's death, the carefully orchestrated sequence was playing out with clockwork precision: January death, May interment, June headstone, and now this - another breadcrumb in a trail spanning generations.

Sam rubbed his eyes, fatigue settling into his bones. Carmichael's declining health had accelerated after their return from Venice last year, his once-brilliant mind deteriorating rapidly even as the global investigation into the Consortium's climate manipulation gained momentum. By November, the man who had orchestrated decades of intelligence operations could barely remember his own grandchildren's names.

Yet somehow, in the midst of that cognitive decline, Carmichael had maintained enough clarity to arrange this elaborate posthumous sequence.

"Sam?" Danielle's voice carried from the hallway. "The cemetery called. The headstone's being installed this morning."

"I'll be right down," he replied, carefully replacing the photograph in its hidden compartment.

Downstairs, he found his family preparing for the day with the coordinated efficiency they'd developed through years of shared purpose. Since Venice, the walls between his operational world and family life had completely dissolved, each member naturally assuming roles that complemented the others.

"Coffee's ready," Danielle said, passing him a steaming mug. At fifty-two, she moved with the grace and confidence of someone who had found her place in a world she once resented. The years of fractured trust after 2011, followed by gradual reconciliation through Paris, Barbados, and Raleigh, had transformed their relationship into something stronger than before.

"Did you sleep at all?" she asked quietly.

Sam shook his head. "Found something else in the saxophone case. A photo collection Carmichael put together - the kids, spanning years. Each showing their particular talents."

"He always saw the patterns," Danielle replied.

"Yeah, but this was different." Sam lowered his voice further. "The earliest photos date back to when they were toddlers, before their abilities would have been obvious. It's like he knew exactly what each of them would become."

Before Danielle could respond, Ellie entered the kitchen, law school acceptance letter in hand. At twenty-three, she carried herself with the composed determination that had made her environmental analysis crucial during the Venice operation.

"Morning," she said, helping herself to coffee. "Ready for Grandpa's headstone installation?"

"As ready as we'll ever be," Sam replied. "Anything from the Institute?"

"Lars called last night. The UN committee has finalized the hearing dates for next month." Ellie didn't need to elaborate on the significance. As the Venice Sphere data continued revealing its secrets, the global implications kept expanding beyond climate manipulation into broader resource control operations.

Rae joined them next, her multilingual greeting mixing French, Italian, and English in the natural flow she'd perfected at twenty-one. Her linguistics studies had evolved far beyond academic interest into operational asset, her ability to decode cultural subtexts proving invaluable during international testimonies.

"Morning, everyone," Cade called out, emerging from the basement where he'd likely been up all night refining algorithms. At eighteen, his programming talents had surpassed even Sam's expectations, creating detection systems that continued identifying remnants of the Consortium's manipulation months after Venice.

Only Mackie, at fifteen, maintained any semblance of normal teenage behavior, trudging into the kitchen with the characteristic morning grumpiness of adolescence. Yet even in his disheveled state, his eyes cataloged the room with the spatial awareness that had unconsciously appeared in his architectural sketches - details that would be invaluable for operational planning.

"Everyone remembers we're meeting at St. Mary's at eleven," Danielle announced, slipping effortlessly into the coordinator role she'd perfected over years of balancing family logistics with security protocols.

"And after?" Mackie asked, reaching for the orange juice.

"Back here," Sam replied. "There's something in Carmichael's saxophone case we need to discuss as a family."

The significance wasn't lost on any of them. Carmichael's saxophone had been more than an instrument - it was a vessel for encrypted communications, mathematical patterns embedded in musical compositions that had guided their operations since Copenhagen.

"Something new?" Cade asked, instantly alert.

"Something that connects everything," Sam answered. "At least, I think it does."

St. Mary's Cemetery on Cumberland Head appeared particularly serene that morning. Ancient maple trees cast dappled shadows across well-tended graves, while the distant hum of the Grand Isle ferry provided a soothing background rhythm. The stone masons had already positioned Carmichael's headstone above his interred ashes, making final adjustments as the family arrived.

CARMICHAEL CAMERON CLAYTON, 1938-2025, followed by a musical staff bearing eight notes—the opening phrase of "Midnight Saxophone," his most famous composition.

"He chose the notes himself?" Rae asked, studying the inscription.

"Specified in his will," Sam confirmed. "Right down to which measures to include."

"It's beautiful," Danielle said softly, placing a small bouquet of blue cornflowers at the base of the stone. "Simple but meaningful."

As the cemetery caretaker finished his work and departed with respectful distance, Sam noticed movement at the cemetery entrance—a figure too deliberately positioned to be a casual visitor.

Another by the small maintenance building. A third near the northern tree line.

His body tensed automatically, and he caught Danielle's eye. The slight nod confirmed she'd noticed the surveillance as well. Years of shared operational awareness had attuned them to the same frequencies.

"Is that who I think it is?" Ellie murmured, her gaze fixed on the figure partially concealed near the northeast corner.

"Roshkov," Sam confirmed quietly.

"First sighting since Rome," Cade noted, casually adjusting his position to better observe the approaches. "That's significant."

"Very," Sam agreed.

Mackie moved closer to his father. "What does he want?"

"That's what we need to find out."

They maintained the appearance of a grieving family paying respects while Sam cataloged every detail of the surveillance operation. Three observers, professionally positioned, with Roshkov directing from partial concealment. Not an immediate threat, but a message being delivered: We're still watching. We're still here.

After a respectful period at the grave, they returned to their vehicles, Sam employing a deliberately indirect route home that would confirm whether they were being actively followed. The techniques that once felt like operational necessity had become natural family protocol, requiring no explanation or instruction. Each member understood their role in maintaining security.

Back at their house on Fjord Drive, Sam secured the property with practiced efficiency while the family gathered in the living room. Carmichael's saxophone case stood propped against the fireplace, its weathered leather containing far more than just an instrument.

"Time to show them what we found," Danielle said, settling beside Sam on the sofa.

Sam nodded, addressing the room. "As you know, your grandfather arranged for his saxophone to be delivered after his burial but before the headstone installation. What you don't know is what I discovered inside last night."

He opened the case carefully, revealing the gleaming brass instrument cradled in faded velvet. Rather than removing it, he pressed specific points along the case's interior, releasing a hidden compartment beneath the main storage area.

From within, he extracted a slim metal device resembling a vintage cigarette case and a sealed envelope bearing Carmichael's distinctive handwriting.

"A data storage device," Cade identified immediately. "Similar technology to what we found in Venice, but older."

"And this," Sam added, opening the envelope to reveal several photographs and a handwritten note. He spread them across the coffee table where everyone could see.

The photographs showed the children at various ages, each captured in moments revealing their particular talents - talents that had proven crucial during the Venice operation and subsequent investigations. The final image showed infant Cade sitting on Carmichael's lap, both examining a saxophone reed with identical expressions of concentration.

"He was tracking our development," Ellie said, picking up a photo of herself at age ten collecting water samples during a family vacation. "Documenting our abilities from the beginning."

"Not just documenting," Sam corrected. "Recognizing patterns that others couldn't see. Your grandfather detected capabilities in each of you that apparently follow specific inheritance lines."

"Like genetic traits?" Cade asked, his scientific curiosity engaged.

"More complex than simple genetics," Danielle explained. "Cognitive development patterns, neural pathways, perceptual abilities that manifest differently in each generation but follow recognizable progressions."

"You're saying Grandpa knew what we'd become before we did," Rae concluded, studying a photo of herself at eight deftly navigating multiple languages during their East Coast trip.

"He saw potential," Sam clarified. "Not destiny. The distinction matters."

"And this?" Mackie asked, pointing to the data device.

Sam exchanged glances with Danielle before continuing. "This contains what appears to be Carmichael's complete operational history - going back decades before I was born. His recruitment, his jazz career as cover, his identification of specific cognitive patterns in certain families, including the Claytons and the Rossis."

"Our mother's family," Danielle added. "My intelligence connections weren't coincidental either."

The revelation settled over the room. While the children had gradually learned about their parents' operational lives since the traumatic events of 2011, this added another layer - their very existence, the union of Sam and Danielle, represented the convergence of cognitive bloodlines Carmichael had identified generations earlier.

"There's more," Sam continued, picking up Carmichael's handwritten note. "This was with the photos."

He read aloud: "The Consortium's climate operation was merely surface level. Four remain hidden. The children are the key to what lies beneath Venice. The music continues between the notes."

"Four Council members remain unidentified," Ellie noted immediately. "We knew that from the Venice data."

"But 'what lies beneath Venice' is new," Cade added. "Another level of the operation we haven't discovered yet."

"And 'the children are the key' refers to us," Rae concluded. "Our specific abilities somehow provide access to whatever remains hidden."

Sam nodded, impressed by their rapid analysis. "According to Carmichael's records, the Consortium's climate manipulation was just one facet of a much larger system. They weren't just controlling climate data for market advantage - they were creating a comprehensive resource control mechanism spanning water rights, agricultural production, energy distribution, and more."

"A perfect information asymmetry," Danielle explained. "They see the real data while everyone else acts on manipulated projections."

Mackie, who had been examining the photos more carefully than the others, looked up with sudden insight. "The patterns in these photos - they're sequential. Like Grandpa was documenting a specific developmental progression in each of us."

Sam felt a surge of pride at his youngest son's observation. "Exactly. Carmichael wasn't just recording your talents; he was identifying how those abilities would manifest at different stages."

"Which means he could predict how they would continue developing," Cade added, the implication dawning on him. "He knew what we'd be capable of now, at our current ages."

"And what we'd need to complete whatever he started," Ellie finished.

The family fell silent, processing the magnitude of this revelation. Their participation in the Venice operation and subsequent investigations hadn't been coincidental - it had been the fulfillment of patterns Carmichael had recognized decades earlier.

"So what now?" Rae finally asked. "What does Carmichael want us to do with this information?"

Sam picked up the data device. "First, we need to examine everything on this drive. Cade, I'll need your help decrypting it. Then we need to understand exactly what 'lies beneath Venice' and how your specific abilities provide access."

"And Roshkov's appearance at the cemetery this morning?" Danielle prompted.

"Suggests the remaining Council members are aware of Carmichael's posthumous instructions," Sam said grimly. "They're watching to see if we find what he left behind."

"Which means we're in danger," Mackie stated matter-of-factly.

"We've been in danger since Copenhagen," Sam replied. "The difference is now we understand why."

Cade had already connected the data device to his laptop and was examining its security protocols. "This uses the same encryption pattern as Carmichael's Midnight Saxophone composition," he observed. "I can access it, but it'll take time."

"How much time?" Ellie asked.

"A few hours, maybe less if I can identify the mathematical sequence correctly." Cade's fingers moved across the keyboard with practiced precision. "The fractal pattern appears to be based on musical intervals unique to jazz improvisation."

"Then get started," Sam directed. "Ellie, contact Lars at the Institute - see if he's made any progress connecting the climate manipulation to broader resource control mechanisms. Rae, we need a comprehensive translation of those Italian documents we recovered from Naples. Mackie, pull together your structural analyses of the Murano facility - there might be something we missed."

The family dispersed to their assignments with the coordinated efficiency of a team that had worked together for years, though their formal operational collaboration dated back only to Venice. Sam watched them go, still processing Carmichael's revelations.

"He orchestrated everything," Danielle said quietly when they were alone. "Our meeting, our children, their abilities... was any of it real, Sam? Or were we just playing parts in Carmichael's grand design?"

Sam turned to her, recognizing the echo of his own doubts. "I've been asking myself the same question since finding those photos. But I've come to believe that Carmichael recognized potential - he didn't create it. He saw patterns and prepared accordingly."

"Not destined. Just prepared," Danielle murmured.

"Exactly. Our choices were our own, even if Carmichael anticipated them. What we built together - our family, our life - that's real, Danielle. It always has been."

She nodded, some of the tension leaving her shoulders. "Even during those hardest years after 2011?"

"Especially then," Sam said. "When everything fell apart, when you discovered my secrets during that East Coast trip... our choice to rebuild, to find a way forward for our children - Carmichael couldn't have engineered that. That was us."

Danielle's smile carried the weight of their shared history - the fracture and gradual healing of a relationship tested by secrecy and deception, but ultimately strengthened through truth. "No more separate worlds," she said, echoing the phrase that had become their mantra since Paris.

"No more separate worlds," Sam agreed, reaching for her hand.

Their moment of connection was interrupted by Cade calling from the basement. "Dad! Mom! I think I've got something!"

They found him in Sam's office, surrounded by multiple screens displaying complex data structures. "I cracked the first layer of encryption," he explained, not looking up from his work. "It's... incredible. Carmichael wasn't just keeping records; he was building a comprehensive map of Consortium operations dating back to the 1950s."

"What kind of map?" Sam asked, leaning over his son's shoulder.

"A personnel network. Financial connections. Resource control mechanisms spanning six continents." Cade highlighted a section of data. "And most importantly, the identities of all twelve Council members, including the four we couldn't identify from the Venice Sphere data."

"That's why Roshkov was at the cemetery," Danielle realized. "They know Carmichael had this information, and they're worried about what happens now that it's in our hands."

"There's more," Cade continued, navigating deeper into the data structure. "The climate manipulation operation was just one branch of their system. They've also been controlling water rights allocations, agricultural production quotas, and energy distribution networks - all using the same mathematical prediction models to create artificial scarcities."

"Creating markets they could control," Sam concluded.

"While maintaining perfect information advantage," Cade confirmed. "They see the real data while everyone else operates on manipulated projections."

"Just like we found in Venice," Danielle said.

"But on a much larger scale," Cade replied. "And with a specific end goal that wasn't clear from the Venice data."

"Which is?" Sam prompted.

Cade looked up, his expression serious. "Total resource dominance. The Consortium isn't just seeking profit - they're positioning themselves to control essential resources during periods of manufactured scarcity."

"Creating crises they can exploit," Danielle interpreted.

"Exactly." Cade returned to his screens. "But here's where it gets even more interesting. Carmichael identified a distinct pattern in how the Council selected its members. Each represents a specific cognitive capability - mathematical modeling, linguistic analysis, environmental interpretation, architectural design..."

"Like our family," Sam said, the realization dawning. "Each of our children's particular talents mirrors a specific Council capability."

"That can't be coincidence," Danielle added.

"According to Carmichael's notes, it's not." Cade indicated another section of data. "He believed certain cognitive patterns appear across generations, clustering in specific family lines. The Council has been tracking these patterns for decades, recruiting or neutralizing individuals with these capabilities."

"Which explains their interest in our children," Sam concluded grimly.

"And why Carmichael was so protective of us," Danielle added. "He wasn't just preparing us for intelligence work; he was shielding us from Council recruitment."

A notification chimed on Cade's laptop as another encryption layer dissolved. "There's something else," he said, studying the newly revealed data.

"Coordinates. Multiple locations worldwide, each associated with what appears to be a resource control node."

"Operational targets," Sam identified immediately.

"But too many for us to address directly," Cade pointed out. "Dozens of locations across six continents."

"We don't need to address them all ourselves," Danielle said. "We just need to expose them, like we did with the Venice Sphere data."

"Exactly," Sam agreed. "If we can provide this information to the same international coalition that handled the climate data exposure, they can coordinate simultaneous operations worldwide."

"But there's one location Carmichael specifically highlighted," Cade noted, indicating a blinking point on the global map. "Deer Island, Upper Saranac Lake."

Sam and Danielle exchanged startled glances. "Bircholm," they said simultaneously.

"The camp?" Cade looked confused. "What would the Consortium want with an Adirondack summer camp?"

Sam felt pieces clicking into place. "Carmichael purchased Bircholm in 2013 without telling anyone. We thought it was just a rental property until his will revealed he'd left it to our family."

"He created a sanctuary," Danielle realized. "Somewhere secure where we could examine this data safely, away from surveillance."

"And according to these coordinates," Cade added, "there's something specific at Bircholm that Carmichael wanted us to find."

The sound of the front door opening announced Ellie and Rae's return. They joined the others in the basement office, expressions indicating they'd made discoveries of their own.

"Lars confirmed unusual activity at multiple climate monitoring stations," Ellie reported. "Pattern shifts that match what we found in the Venice data, but more subtle. The Consortium is adapting their methods."

"And the Italian documents are more significant than we initially thought," Rae added. "They don't just detail historical climate records; they contain references to something called 'La Sfera di Controllo' - the Sphere of Control."

"Which appears to be broader than the Venice Sphere we recovered," Ellie continued. "Lars believes it's a comprehensive system for monitoring and manipulating global resource distribution."

"That aligns with what we've found in Carmichael's data," Sam said, gesturing to Cade's screens. "The climate operation was just one component of a much larger system."

"And Bircholm somehow connects to all of this," Danielle added.

Mackie appeared in the doorway, architectural sketches in hand. "I've been reviewing the Murano facility blueprints," he announced. "There's a structural anomaly I missed before - a section beneath the main vault that doesn't appear on any official plans."

"Something beneath Venice," Sam quoted from Carmichael's note. "The final piece of the puzzle."

"So we have two critical locations," Danielle summarized. "Something hidden at Bircholm and something concealed beneath the Murano facility in Venice."

"And four remaining Council members still unidentified," Ellie added.

"Not anymore," Cade corrected, turning his screen to show profile dossiers. "Carmichael's data includes complete identifications. Four individuals controlling sovereign wealth funds with combined assets exceeding two trillion dollars."

The family fell silent, absorbing the magnitude of this revelation. They had exposed the Consortium's climate manipulation through the Venice operation, but Carmichael's posthumous guidance revealed a much larger target.

"We need to go to Bircholm," Sam decided. "Whatever Carmichael hid there could be crucial to understanding the full scope of the Consortium's operations."

"And we need to alert the international coalition about the remaining Council members," Danielle added.

"What about Roshkov?" Rae asked. "His appearance at the cemetery this morning wasn't coincidental."

"No," Sam agreed. "He's sending a message. He knows about Carmichael's data and wants us to understand that the Council is watching."

"Is he warning us or threatening us?" Ellie wondered.

"With Roshkov, it's usually both," Sam replied. "Either way, we need to move quickly. If he knows about Carmichael's posthumous instructions, others do as well."

"When do we leave for Bircholm?" Cade asked.

Sam checked his watch. "Tomorrow morning. Everyone pack essential equipment only. Standard security protocols."

As the family dispersed to prepare, Sam remained in his office, studying the data Cade had unlocked. The scope of Carmichael's operation was breathtaking - a decades-long mission tracking the Consortium's evolution from post-war economic influencers to global resource manipulators. And somehow, his father had recognized that Sam's children would possess the specific capabilities needed to counter the Council's operations.

Not destiny. Preparation.

Later that evening, after the house had quieted, Sam found Danielle on the back deck, gazing across Lake Champlain toward the distant mountains. The sunset painted the landscape in shades of amber and gold, creating a moment of tranquility before tomorrow's departure.

"Are you sure about this?" she asked as he joined her. "Bringing the children deeper into this world?"

"They're already part of it," Sam replied. "Have been since birth, apparently. The question isn't whether to involve them, but how to protect them while acknowledging their capabilities."

"I never imagined our family vacation spot would turn out to be part of some grand intelligence operation," Danielle said with a slight smile. "Though I suppose I should have guessed, given Carmichael's involvement."

"He created a sanctuary for us," Sam said. "Somewhere we could be together, safe from surveillance, while continuing the work he began."

"The work he prepared our children to complete," Danielle added, her expression growing serious. "Are you worried about what we'll find at Bircholm?"

"Yes," Sam admitted. "But I'm more concerned about what happens afterward. Exposing the remaining Council members, revealing the full scope of their resource control operations - it changes everything we thought we accomplished in Venice."

"And puts us squarely in their sights again," Danielle concluded.

"Us and the children," Sam confirmed grimly. "But Carmichael believed they were ready. That their specific abilities would provide access to whatever lies beneath Venice."

"Not destined," Danielle quoted. "Just prepared."

"Exactly." Sam reached for her hand. "Whatever Carmichael arranged, whatever he saw in our children's futures, the choices remain ours. We decide how far to go, how much risk to accept."

"As a family," Danielle emphasized. "No more separate worlds."

"No more separate worlds," Sam agreed.

As darkness settled over Cumberland Head, the distant lights of the Grand Isle ferry created a shimmering path across the water - a reminder of connections spanning distance, of journeys between separate shores. Tomorrow they would travel to Bircholm, following Carmichael's final guidance toward whatever he had hidden at Deer Island.

The breeze carried the faint sound of saxophone music from Cade's room - not Carmichael's encoded Midnight Saxophone, but something new, something original. His own composition, finding melody in the spaces between inherited patterns.

Sam smiled, recognizing the perfect metaphor. Whatever Carmichael had prepared, whatever patterns he had recognized across generations, the music their family created remained uniquely their own. Not destined, but composed note by note through their own choices.

Tomorrow would bring new challenges as they continued unraveling the Consortium's operations. But tonight, in this moment between movements, Sam found unexpected peace. The balance he'd sought for decades—between teaching and operations, between family and duty—suddenly seemed possible.

"Listen," Danielle said softly, tilting her head toward Cade's music drifting through the open window.

"He's good," Sam replied. "Creating something new from what Carmichael left behind."

"Just like all of us," Danielle observed.

The music continued, filling the space between past and future with possibilities only they could create.

Chapter 12
The Final Resolution
July-August 2025

Sunrise painted the Adirondacks in amber light as Sam guided the Rinker Cuddy away from shore. Dawn reflections danced across Upper Saranac Lake's surface, creating a shimmering path toward their destination. Behind them, the Wawbeek landing receded into the distance as they headed toward Deer Island, following the coordinates Carmichael had embedded in his final instructions.

"Beautiful morning," Danielle remarked beside him, her chestnut curls lifted by the breeze. Six months since Carmichael's passing, she had found unexpected peace in the revelations that followed – discovering that her mother's intelligence connections mirrored Sam's family legacy, that their marriage had united cognitive bloodlines Carmichael had identified decades earlier. In the boat's stern, their children maintained a relaxed vigilance that had become second nature.

Ellie adjusted her sunglasses while reviewing law school materials, multitasking even during this critical family mission. Rae hummed softly, her distinctive voice carrying across the water as she scanned the shoreline with practiced casualness. Cade monitored the boat's instruments with unnecessary attention, his fingers occasionally tapping complex patterns against the console. Beside him, Mackie sketched the approaching shoreline, capturing details most would miss.

"Everyone clear on what we're looking for?" Sam asked, navigating the Rinker around a submerged rock formation visible only to experienced eyes.

No one answered directly – they didn't need to. The briefing before departure had covered everything: Carmichael's coordinates pointing to a specific location on Deer Island; the probability of hidden information connecting to the "Sphere of Control" mentioned in the Italian documents; the need for each family member's unique perceptual abilities to access whatever lay waiting at Bircholm.

Sam couldn't help smiling at how naturally they'd adapted to this shared purpose. What had once been his greatest secret, the operational life he'd hidden from his family for decades, had transformed into their collective mission – bridging the divide that had fractured their world after Danielle's traumatic discovery in 2011.

"Still can't believe this place is actually ours," Cade commented as Deer Island grew larger before them, its pine-covered slopes rising from the water like a sentinel.

"Technically, it's been ours for years," Mackie corrected. "We just didn't know it."

The observation carried deeper truth than mere property ownership. Bircholm represented Carmichael's foresight – a sanctuary purchased secretly in 2013, maintained through elaborate cover as a rental property, then revealed as the family's inheritance only after his death. A truth hidden in plain sight, just like the talents he'd recognized in his grandchildren before they were fully evident.

As they approached the familiar southern boathouse, Sam reduced speed. The massive timber structure had stood since 1887, its weathered beams having witnessed generations of Adirondack summers. Now it would serve as entry point to whatever

Carmichael had concealed at these precise coordinates.

"Standard security sweep before unpacking," Danielle directed as Sam guided the boat into the shadowed interior. Though phrased as vacation routine, every family member understood the operational subtext – verifying the property remained secure after months of absence.

The family moved with coordinated efficiency as they disembarked and gathered supplies. Years of shared experience had created an operational shorthand requiring no explicit instruction. Ellie and Rae automatically positioned themselves to monitor approach vectors while Cade and Mackie unloaded equipment with practiced care.

"You feeling nostalgic?" Danielle asked quietly, noticing Sam's gaze lingering on the boathouse structure.

"Thinking about Carmichael," he admitted. "All those summers he arranged for us to rent this place, never letting on he actually owned it. Creating memories here while positioning us exactly where he needed us to be."

"Not manipulating," Danielle corrected gently. "Preparing."

Sam nodded, accepting the distinction that had become increasingly important as they unraveled Carmichael's posthumous guidance. The difference between destiny and preparation, between orchestrating their lives and recognizing their potential – it was a line his father had walked with remarkable precision.

The family made their way up the sloping path toward the main lodge, each automatically scanning their surroundings with the situational awareness that had become second nature. Deer Island rose gradually from the shoreline, white pines towering over the collection of shingled buildings that comprised Bircholm. The main lodge stood at the heart of the compound, surrounded by smaller cabins and outbuildings connected by winding paths.

Inside the main lodge, sunlight streamed through multi-paned windows, illuminating the great room with its massive stone fireplace and hand-hewn beams. The space smelled of pine, cedar, and memories – both those they'd already created during years of family vacations and those yet to be made in their new understanding of Bircholm's significance.

"Everyone settle in and meet back here in thirty minutes," Danielle directed. "We need to review the coordinates again before beginning the search."

Sam made his way to the master bedroom overlooking the lake, the familiar space holding new significance now that they understood Carmichael had created this sanctuary specifically for them. He placed his bag on the cedar chest at the foot of the bed, then retrieved the data device they'd discovered in the saxophone case.

"Need a minute?" Danielle asked from the doorway, reading his expression with the insight of thirty years together.

"Just getting my bearings," Sam replied, tucking the device into his pocket. "Knowing why Carmichael brought us here changes everything about how I see this place."

She crossed to him, resting her head against his shoulder. "I've been thinking about what you said before we left home. About turning down the committee position."

The International Climate Data Oversight Committee had practically begged Sam to chair their newly formed organization. With his unique combination of scientific credentials and firsthand knowledge of the Consortium's manipulation, he was the obvious choice to lead global reform efforts.

"Teaching is where I belong," Sam said simply. "Always has been."

"Even knowing what we know now? That Carmichael and Marcus guided you toward that career from the beginning?"

Sam considered this, a question that had haunted him since discovering the extent of his father's orchestration. "Their influence doesn't make my passion any less authentic. If anything, Carmichael recognized something genuine in me and helped it flourish."

"Like you've done with our children," Danielle observed.

The parallel wasn't lost on Sam. He'd guided each child's natural talents without forcing predetermined paths. Ellie's environmental advocacy, Rae's linguistic gifts, Cade's technical brilliance, and Mackie's spatial intelligence had all developed organically, even as they aligned perfectly with the capabilities needed to counter the Consortium's operations.

"We should join the others," Sam suggested after a moment.

Downstairs, their children had assembled in the great room, each already focused on aspects of their shared mission. Ellie stood by the massive windows, finishing a call with Lars Johannsen from the Institute. Rae sat in an oversized chair, notebook open as she refined translations of the Italian documents. Cade occupied the window seat, laptop balanced on his knees as he analyzed the coordinate patterns Carmichael had left them. Mackie sprawled on the hearth rug, creating a detailed three-dimensional rendering of Bircholm's structure based on the original blueprints they'd discovered.

"Before we begin," Sam started, drawing everyone's attention, "we should acknowledge what we've accomplished over the past six months."

"And what still remains to be done," Ellie added with characteristic focus.

Sam nodded. "Since Venice, the evidence we uncovered has led to eleven arrests, regulatory overhaul of climate data collection protocols, and UN sanctions against Consortium-affiliated organizations."

"But Kessler remains free," Cade pointed out, voicing their shared frustration.

"For now," Danielle agreed. "Though the Council exposure has limited his influence significantly."

"And Marcus believes it's just a matter of time," Sam assured them. "The remaining Council members can't hide forever, especially with the information from Carmichael's data device."

No one questioned how Sam maintained contact with Marcus Cartier, officially declared dead three years ago. Some operational details remained compartmentalized, even within their increasingly transparent family structure.

"I've been thinking about Roshkov," Rae said, shifting the conversation. "His appearance at Grandpa's headstone installation wasn't coincidental."

Ivan Roshkov's role as double agent within the Consortium had proven crucial to their success in Venice. His subsequent disappearance had surprised no one, though his cryptic parting message about serving "the same entity your father served" continued to puzzle them.

"Nothing Roshkov does is coincidental," Sam agreed. "His presence at the cemetery signals the Council knows about Carmichael's posthumous instructions."

"Which means they might know about this place too," Mackie concluded, glancing up from his sketches.

"Possible, but unlikely," Danielle said. "Carmichael maintained this property through multiple shell companies. Even the real estate records we found listed a holding corporation in Liechtenstein as the owner."

Cade looked up from his laptop. "According to these coordinates, what we're looking for is somewhere beneath the main lodge. The measurements indicate a space approximately twenty feet below the stone foundation."

"That would put it below the water table," Ellie pointed out. "Unless there's some kind of waterproofing system we don't know about."

"Grandpa wouldn't have gone to all this trouble for nothing," Rae reasoned. "If he specified these coordinates, something's down there."

"Mackie," Sam said, turning to his youngest, "your spatial analysis of the original blueprints—did you find any structural anomalies?"

Mackie flipped through his sketches, pulling out a detailed cross-section of the main lodge. "There's a discrepancy between the foundation depth shown on the 1887 plans and what appears on the renovation permits from the 1950s. The original foundation extends about fifteen feet deeper than what's listed on later documents."

"Hidden in plain sight," Sam murmured. "Documenting a shallower foundation to conceal whatever's beneath."

"But how do we access it?" Danielle asked. "There's no obvious entrance point."

"If I were designing a hidden chamber," Mackie said, his architectural mind engaged, "I'd want an access route that seemed natural to the structure. Something that wouldn't attract attention even if someone was looking specifically for irregularities."

"The fireplace," Cade suggested, eyeing the massive stone hearth dominating the great room.

"Too obvious," Mackie countered. "And the thermal signature would make it easy to detect with modern scanning equipment."

"The boat house," Ellie said suddenly. "It's the oldest structure on the property, and it's partially below water level already. A perfect access point for something deeper."

Cade cross-referenced the coordinates. "That fits. If you calculate a thirty-degree angle from the boat house toward the main lodge, it aligns perfectly with the location Carmichael specified."

"A tunnel?" Danielle asked.

"More likely an access shaft," Sam suggested. "Something narrow and direct, possibly disguised as part of the original dock pilings."

They returned to the boat house, examining the structure with fresh understanding. What had appeared as a simple lakeside storage facility now revealed subtle indicators of its dual purpose— timber beams spaced at mathematically precise intervals, floor planking that created an almost imperceptible pattern when viewed from certain angles.

"There," Mackie said, pointing to a section of wall behind where they'd moored the boat. "The support beams are arranged in a fibonacci sequence. Classic Carmichael."

Sam examined the wall carefully, running his fingers along the weathered wood. "Good catch. But how does it open?"

Cade approached, studying the pattern with the same mathematical precision that had made him invaluable during the Venice operation. "If it follows Grandpa's usual encryption methods, the access mechanism would respond to a specific sequence."

"Like musical intervals," Rae suggested. "The same pattern we found in his Midnight Saxophone composition."

Cade nodded, pressing specific points along the beams in a pattern that mirrored the opening notes of Carmichael's signature piece. Nothing happened.

"Maybe it's not that literal," Ellie suggested. "Grandpa was always telling us to think beyond the obvious, to see the spaces between notes."

Sam considered this, recalling Carmichael's favorite phrase. "The music continues between the notes." He studied the wall again, this time focusing not on the beams themselves but on the spaces between them.

"Try the negative space," he suggested to Cade. "The intervals between the pressure points, not the points themselves."

Cade adjusted his approach, applying pressure to different spots that corresponded to the pauses between notes in Carmichael's composition. A soft click rewarded his effort, and a section of wall shifted inward before sliding aside, revealing a narrow passage beyond.

"Of course," Danielle said. "It's not the notes, but the spaces between them."

They retrieved flashlights from their equipment and entered the passage one by one. The tunnel was surprisingly modern—reinforced concrete walls, recessed lighting that activated automatically, and a slight downward slope leading beneath the island.

"This wasn't built in the 1880s," Ellie observed, examining the construction. "This is recent work."

"Carmichael renovated the entire property in 2013," Sam recalled. "Must have added this during the construction."

The passage continued for nearly two hundred feet, gradually descending before terminating at a sealed door resembling a bank vault. A digital keypad glowed softly beside it, waiting for the correct entry code.

"Another security layer," Cade noted, examining the system. "Biometric, probably keyed to specific family members."

"Try your hand," Sam suggested to his son. "Carmichael mentioned the children being the key."

Cade placed his palm against the scanner. The system hummed briefly before flashing red. "Rejected."

Each family member tried in turn, with identical results. The system recognized them—confirmed by personalized rejection messages—but required something more specific than mere identity verification.

"It's asking for a sequence," Rae observed, studying the display messages more carefully. "Not just recognition, but recognition in a specific order."

"The order Carmichael documented our abilities," Ellie suggested. "In his photographs and notes."

Sam considered this. "Chronological development, maybe? The sequence our abilities manifested?"

"Ellie first," Danielle said. "Her environmental awareness appeared earliest."

Ellie placed her palm on the scanner again. This time, the system flashed yellow rather than red.

"Progress," she noted. "Who was next?"

"Rae's linguistic facilities," Sam recalled. "You were switching between languages effortlessly by age five."

Rae's palm against the scanner produced another yellow confirmation.

"Then Cade," Danielle continued. "His mathematical patterns were evident by seven."

Cade's scan yielded a third yellow light.

"And Mackie last," Sam concluded. "His spatial awareness became obvious around nine."

When Mackie completed the sequence, the system flashed green and the vault door released with a pneumatic hiss, swinging silently inward to reveal a chamber beyond.

Inside, they found not the treasure vault or weapons cache that might be expected from such elaborate security, but a simple, modern office. A desk dominated the center, supporting multiple computer terminals. Bookshelves lined the walls, filled with research materials spanning decades. A comfortable sitting area occupied one corner, while another held what appeared to be a small recording studio.

"Carmichael's sanctuary," Sam said quietly, taking in the space that so perfectly reflected his father's dual nature—musician and operative, artist and analyst.

"Look at this," Ellie called, examining one terminal that had activated upon their entry. The screen displayed a welcome message addressed specifically to them:

"To my family—If you're reading this, you've successfully navigated my final guidance. What follows is the culmination of fifty years tracking the organization now known as the Consortium. Their climate operation that you exposed in Venice represents merely the surface level of a much more ambitious system—one designed to control essential resources during periods of manufactured scarcity."

The message continued, detailing Carmichael's decades-long investigation that had begun during the Cold War and evolved as he recognized patterns connecting seemingly unrelated global developments—financial market manipulations, academic research suppression, strategic resource acquisitions, and technological control mechanisms.

"The remaining four Council members represent the system's cornerstone," Carmichael's message explained. "Where identified members controlled implementation, these individuals design strategy. Their exposure is necessary but insufficient. The Venice Sphere you recovered contains operational data, but the true control mechanism—what I've termed the Sphere of Control—remains hidden beneath the Murano facility in a chamber your initial operation didn't detect."

"A secondary level beneath the vault we accessed," Mackie realized, recalling the structural anomaly he'd identified in the facility blueprints.

"Exactly what the Italian documents referred to," Rae added. "'La Sfera di Controllo'—not just a concept but a physical control system."

Carmichael's message proceeded to outline the capabilities this system contained—artificial intelligence algorithms designed to predict and manipulate global resource distribution, quantum encryption protecting the Council's true financial assets, and most disturbing, a deadman switch designed to implement catastrophic market manipulations if the system were compromised.

"This explains why we detected unusual activity after Venice," Cade said. "The remaining Council members are preparing to activate contingency protocols."

"Which would trigger artificial scarcities in essential resources," Ellie concluded.

The final section of Carmichael's message shifted from operational to personal:

"I've watched each of you develop capabilities I recognized in myself and in your mother's family, Danielle. These weren't abilities I created but patterns I identified—cognitive frameworks that manifest differently in each generation but follow recognizable progressions. The Council has tracked similar patterns for decades, recruiting or neutralizing individuals with these capabilities.

"Your children represent something unique—the convergence of multiple cognitive bloodlines, enhanced by the educational environment you created. Not destiny but preparation. The choices remain yours, always. But the potential I recognized has flowered into capabilities perfectly suited to counter what the Council has built.

"The coordinates for the Sphere of Control are included in the attached files. Marcus will provide necessary support for the operation. Trust Roshkov only when verification is possible.

"I regret that I won't see the completion of what we've begun together. Know that everything I've done—every manipulation, every secret kept, every path subtly directed—came from love and the desire to protect what truly matters. Not just family, but the principles family exists to preserve.

"The music continues between the notes. Find harmony in the spaces where you write your own composition.

"—Carmichael"

Silence fell as they absorbed their grandfather's final message. Sam felt the weight of decades of planning—his father's intricate design spanning generations, recognizing patterns others couldn't see, preparing them for this moment without determining their choices.

"There's more," Cade said, examining additional files that had unlocked with Carmichael's message. "Complete dossiers on the remaining Council members, access protocols for the Sphere of Control, and contingency plans for neutralizing the deadman switch."

"He thought of everything," Danielle murmured.

"Not everything," Sam corrected gently. "He prepared what he could, but left the execution to us. Our choices, our implementation."

"So what do we do?" Ellie asked, looking to her parents.

Sam exchanged glances with Danielle before responding. "We complete what Carmichael started. We expose the remaining Council members, neutralize the Sphere of Control, and prevent the activation of their contingency protocols."

"But this time, we do it together," Danielle added. "Not as Carmichael's pawns but as partners implementing his preparation."

"I've been thinking about that," Rae said. "About patterns and preparation versus destiny. If Grandpa could see all this in us from the beginning, were our choices ever really our own?"

"I've asked myself that same question since finding his data device," Sam admitted. "But I've come to believe that Carmichael recognized potential rather than created it. He saw patterns and prepared accordingly."

"Not destined," Ellie quoted. "Just prepared."

"Exactly," Sam agreed. "Your interests, your talents —they're genuinely yours. Carmichael simply ensured you'd have opportunities to develop them."

"Like you and Mom did for us," Cade observed.

"We tried," Sam said with a smile. "Though with considerably less foresight than Carmichael apparently possessed."

Further exploration of the underground facility revealed additional resources Carmichael had assembled—specialized equipment for the Venice operation he'd anticipated, secure communication systems linked to Marcus's network, and comprehensive research materials documenting the Consortium's evolution over fifty years.

As evening approached, they returned to the main lodge, each processing Carmichael's revelations differently. Danielle prepared dinner while the children organized the information they'd discovered, preparing for what would clearly be a significant operation to complete what they'd begun in Venice.

The sound of a saxophone drifted through the lodge as Cade practiced in the music room, the notes of "Midnight Saxophone" carrying new significance now that they understood its dual purpose—both beautiful music and sophisticated encryption.

Sam found himself on the dock, watching the sunset paint Upper Saranac Lake in shades of gold and crimson. The serenity of Bircholm contrasted sharply with the global implications of what they'd discovered, yet both felt equally part of his reality now.

Footsteps on the wooden planks announced Ellie's approach. His eldest daughter joined him at the dock's edge, their reflections merging in the water below.

"You're really going back to just teaching?" she asked without preamble.

Sam smiled at her directness. "Nothing 'just' about teaching, Ellie."

"You know what I mean. After everything we've discovered, everything we've done."

"That's precisely why I'm returning to the classroom," Sam explained. "The next generation needs educators who understand the difference between data and manipulation, between science and agenda."

Ellie considered this. "Like you taught us."

"I tried."

"You succeeded," she assured him. "Even before we knew about your other work. You always taught us to question, to verify, to look beyond the obvious."

Sam felt unexpected emotion tighten his throat. Despite all the operational successes of the past year, this simple affirmation from his daughter meant more.

"What about you?" he asked after composing himself. "Law school starts in a month."

"I'm going," Ellie confirmed. "Environmental law is more important than ever with what we know now. But I'm also meeting with the Institute's legal team next week."

She paused, seemingly uncertain how to continue.

"You've been offered a position," Sam guessed.

She nodded. "Research consultant during school. They want someone who understands both the science and the legal implications of the Consortium's actions."

"Sounds perfect for you."

"It would mean staying involved," she pointed out. "Not just with climate science, but with the ongoing investigations."

"The middle path," Sam said, echoing their earlier conversation. "Professional development aligned with genuine interests, but connected to the larger mission."

Ellie smiled. "Exactly."

A comfortable silence settled between them as they watched a heron glide across the lake, wings barely disturbing the water's surface.

"Dad," Ellie said eventually, her tone shifting to something more tentative. "Do you ever wonder if we would have developed these interests and abilities without Grandpa's influence? If he somehow shaped us to fit roles he'd already designed?"

The question echoed Sam's own doubts since discovering Carmichael's underground office. "I've thought about that constantly," he admitted. "But I've come to believe he recognized potential rather than created it. He saw patterns in all of you and prepared accordingly."

"Like you and Mom did," Ellie said.

"With less orchestration but equal love," Sam replied.

The sound of Cade's saxophone shifted to a new melody—not Carmichael's composition but something original, notes flowing with youthful creativity while building on classical foundations.

"That's beautiful," Ellie commented. "I don't recognize it."

"It's his own," Sam said proudly. "The next generation taking what came before and making it their own."

Inside the main lodge, they found the rest of the family gathering for dinner. The dining table had been set with Carmichael's antique silver and crystal that he'd stored at Bircholm, transforming a simple meal into a celebration. Delicious aromas filled the space as Danielle emerged from the kitchen carrying her signature lasagna.

"Perfect timing," she said, spotting Sam and Ellie. "Cade, that's enough practice for now."

The saxophone notes faded as their son appeared from the music room, instrument still in hand. "I think I've figured out the third movement's pattern," he said, the comment holding dual meaning—both musical interpretation and encryption analysis.

"After dinner," Sam suggested. "Some things shouldn't be rushed."

As they gathered around the table, conversations blended operational planning with genuine family connection. Rae discussed translation nuances in the Italian documents while helping Mackie with his French homework. Ellie outlined environmental law precedents relevant to their case while Cade explained his decryption progress. The boundaries that had once separated family life from operational necessity had dissolved completely, creating a new synthesis that felt both natural and powerful.

Sam raised his glass. "To family."

Simple words, but they encompassed everything— their shared journey, their integrated purpose, their uncertain but promising future.

"And to Grandpa," Mackie added. "Who saw patterns the rest of us missed."

"To Carmichael," they echoed.

Later, as darkness settled over Deer Island, they gathered on the main lodge's expansive porch. Stars emerged above the pines, more visible here than at their Cumberland Head home. In the distance, loons called across the water, their haunting cries echoing through the Adirondack night.

Cade approached, carrying Carmichael's saxophone case. Inside lay not only the instrument but the legacy it represented—both musical and operational.

"I've been thinking," he said, opening the case with careful reverence. "About what Grandpa said in his final message—about music continuing between the notes."

"What about it?" Sam asked.

"It applies to more than just his compositions," Cade explained. "It's about what happens next—the spaces we create after resolving one phrase before beginning another."

Sam reflected on the metaphor. Their exposure of the Consortium's climate operation represented a completed musical phrase, but the composition continued. The space between—this moment at Bircholm—provided essential breathing room before the next movement began.

"We're in that space now," Danielle observed, following the metaphor. "Between what we've accomplished and what comes next."

"And we get to compose the next section ourselves," Cade concluded, lifting the saxophone from its case.

The instrument gleamed in the porch light, its brass surfaces reflecting their gathered faces. This saxophone had carried Carmichael's encrypted messages, guided their operations, and now served as symbol of their shared future.

"Play something," Mackie suggested from his position on the porch steps.

Cade hesitated. "Not Midnight Saxophone. Something new."

He raised the instrument and began playing—not Carmichael's composition with its embedded codes, but an original melody. The notes drifted across the water, clear and unencumbered by hidden meanings.

As the impromptu concert continued, Sam slipped his arm around Danielle's waist. "We did it," he whispered. "Protected their future while honoring the past."

On the lake beyond, moonlight created a silver path across the water's surface. The same moon that had illuminated their operations in Copenhagen, Paris, Barbados, Raleigh, and Venice now shone on this peaceful moment.

Cade's saxophone notes faded into the night, leaving a momentary silence broken only by gentle waves against the shoreline.

"I found something else," he said, returning the instrument to its case. From beneath the velvet lining, he withdrew an envelope that hadn't been there before.

Sam recognized the handwriting immediately. "When did that appear?"

"This afternoon," Cade admitted. "When I was practicing in the music room. It wasn't there when we arrived."

The implication hung in the air. Someone had accessed Bircholm during their brief absence, leaving this message in a location only family would find.

Sam accepted the envelope, examining its unmarked exterior before carefully opening it. Inside lay a single sheet of paper containing just three lines:

The council fragment remains. The music never truly ends. -M

"Marcus," Ellie whispered, reading over his shoulder.

The message confirmed what they'd suspected—their work wasn't complete. Despite exposing most of the Council, elements remained operational. And Marcus, despite his supposed death, continued the mission.

"Do we show this to Lars?" Rae asked, practical as always.

Sam considered the question, weighing transparency against operational security. "Tomorrow," he decided. "Tonight belongs to family."

He carefully returned the note to its envelope and placed it in his pocket. This new information would shape their path forward, but it needn't disrupt this hard-earned moment of peace.

Cade reclaimed the saxophone, playing a softer melody that blended with the natural sounds of the Adirondack night. Rae hummed harmony, her voice finding the spaces between notes with instinctive precision.

As the music surrounded them, Sam reflected on their journey. What had begun as his isolated operation had transformed into a shared family purpose. The skills Carmichael had recognized in each of them had proven crucial not just for intelligence work, but for their collective strength.

The revelation that Sam's recruitment had been orchestrated by Carmichael no longer felt like manipulation. Instead, it represented his father's insight—recognizing patterns and preparing accordingly. Not destiny, but preparation.

"Penny for your thoughts," Danielle murmured beside him.

Sam watched his children—Cade playing, Rae singing, Ellie and Mackie listening with identical expressions of contentment.

"Just appreciating this moment," he replied. "Between the notes."

Danielle squeezed his hand in understanding. "We'll face tomorrow's challenges together."

"No more separate worlds," Sam agreed, their shared mantra now a family truth.

On the lake beyond Bircholm, a loon called into the darkness—solitary yet connected to the water, the night, the endless cycle of seasons. Sam felt a similar paradox within himself—individual purpose integrated with family legacy, operational necessity balanced with genuine connection.

As Cade's melody concluded, silence settled over Deer Island once again. Not an ending, but a pause between movements in their continuing composition.

Tomorrow would bring new challenges—Marcus's message, Lars's revelations, and the remnants of the

Consortium's operations. But tonight, under the Adirondack stars, the Clayton family had found harmony between the complex music of their shared purpose and the simple melody of being together.

Sam's decision to return to teaching rather than pursue international committees suddenly felt more right than ever. His classroom represented the perfect bridge between his operational knowledge and his educational calling—the ideal space to guide the next generation toward truth in a world of manipulation.

Throughout decades of living divided lives, Sam had always felt pulled between competing purposes. Now, those purposes had aligned. Teaching wasn't separate from his mission against the Consortium—it was essential to it.

As his family gradually dispersed to their respective cabins, Sam remained on the porch, savoring the night sounds and the knowledge that Carmichael had created this sanctuary specifically for them. Bircholm wasn't just a family retreat; it was the physical embodiment of his father's legacy—beautiful, enduring, and designed to shelter those he loved most.

Danielle joined him for a final moment before retiring. "Coming to bed?"

"In a minute," he promised. "Just taking it all in."

After she'd gone, Sam retrieved the envelope from his pocket, reading Marcus's cryptic message once more.

The council fragment remains. The music never truly ends. -M

The first line warned of continued threat. The second offered both challenge and promise—their work would continue, as would their family's legacy.

Sam carefully returned the note to his pocket. Tomorrow would be time enough to analyze its implications and plan their next movements. Tonight belonged to the space between notes—to reflection, to family, to the harmony they'd found amidst global discord.

Inside Carmichael's saxophone case, nestled beneath the velvet lining, lay another reed— unmarked, unencrypted, waiting for new music to bring it to life. Not a message from the past, but an invitation to the future.

Sam closed the case gently, securing its latches with practiced hands. Whatever came next, they would face it together—teacher and operatives, parents and children, individuals and family. No more separate worlds.

The loon called once more across the water, a solitary note perfect in its simplicity. Sam smiled and turned toward the warmth of the lodge, leaving the porch to darkness and possibility.

The music would continue, but tonight's melody had reached its perfect cadence.